CORBIN

The Mavericks, Book 17

Dale Mayer

CORBIN: THE MAVERICKS, BOOK 17
Beverly Dale Mayer
Valley Publishing Ltd.

Copyright © 2022

This is a work of fiction. Names, characters, places, brands, media, and incidents are either the product of the author's imagination or are used fictitiously. Any resemblance to actual events, locales, or persons, living or dead, is entirely coincidental.

ISBN-13: 978-1-773365-39-8
Print Edition

Books in This Series:

Kerrick, Book 1

Griffin, Book 2

Jax, Book 3

Beau, Book 4

Asher, Book 5

Ryker, Book 6

Miles, Book 7

Nico, Book 8

Keane, Book 9

Lennox, Book 10

Gavin, Book 11

Shane, Book 12

Diesel, Book 13

Jerricho, Book 14

Killian, Book 15

Hatch, Book 16

Corbin, Book 17

Aiden, Book 18

Boxed Sets and Bundles

https://geni.us/Bundlepage

About This Book

What happens when the very men—trained to make the hard decisions—come up against the rules and regulations that hold them back from doing what needs to be done? They either stay and work within the constraints given to them or they walk away. Only now, for a select few, they have another option:

The Mavericks. A covert black ops team that steps up and break all the rules … but gets the job done.

Welcome to a new military romance series by *USA Today* best-selling author Dale Mayer. A series where you meet new friends and just might get to meet old ones too in this raw and compelling look at the men who keep us safe every day from the darkness where they operate—and live—in the shadows … until someone special helps them step into the light.

Corbin is tracking a cabinet minister's pregnant daughter, who'd been snatched off the streets several days ago. The incident followed several other missing women's cases, except those women already had given birth, and their children were also kidnapped at the same time. Then the body of one of the mothers is found …

Nellie would do anything to save her unborn child, but finding herself a prisoner was never something she expected to happen. When one of her guards grills her over an image of someone asking questions about her, she realizes she isn't as alone as she'd assumed. Now if only a rescue could be mounted before any others die …

A rescue is one thing, but getting to the bottom of this nightmare becomes even more urgent, as the kidnapper refuses to give up on Nellie's unborn child and the big payoff if he succeeds …

Sign up to be notified of all Dale's releases here!
https://geni.us/DaleNews

PROLOGUE

CORBIN WALLACE ENTERED his hotel room, worn out and ready for some rest, after the successful end to his recent op with Hatch.

He read the message from Hatch on his phone, telling Corbin to stay on his side of the adjoining rooms, and he laughed out loud. "Well, Hatch, you called it, and Millie's all yours, but, dammit, I want the next one." With all the pressure of the last few days now resolved, Corbin crashed and slept through the night.

When he got up the next morning, he found more messages from Jonas at MI6, and Corbin knew that the next few days would be crazy busy.

He saw Millie and Hatch a couple times, but they were clearly in a world of their own, and Corbin was so happy for them. By the time he was done with MI6 and had a chance to catch up with the happy couple, Corbin looked over at Hatch and asked, "So, will you stay here for now?"

"Yeah, I will," he confirmed. "How are you doing? Is your arm okay?"

"Yeah, the bullet went a little deeper than I realized, but I'm good. Just worn out, but a few days of rest will be good for me."

"Well, hopefully that is something you get," Hatch noted, "but, as usual, there are never any guarantees."

"I know. Apparently the next job is just around the corner."

"It is," Hatch confirmed. "Sounds like I'll be your handler. Although I'm not sure how long the Mavericks' department will function. The focus is changing I believe, the brass being what they are."

Corbin smiled. "In the meantime, I presume you'll be handling it from here?"

"Absolutely, since I have a reason to stay close." He watched as Millie neared, and, when he held out his hand, Millie immediately grabbed on to it and smiled back.

"I'll help MI6 go through all the contents of the warehouse." She looked over at Corbin. "I suspect it'll take a few weeks."

He laughed. "Are you kidding? That'll take a few months." But he turned to Hatch and added, "Just give me a couple days to recuperate, if you can."

"If I can. And then we'll figure out where you're going."

"Maybe nowhere," Corbin suggested. "Maybe it'll be nice and calm, and we'll just stay here in England."

"Hey, it's possible," Hatch admitted, "and I'm not against that at all."

"Good," Corbin murmured. "Give me a couple days, and then we'll talk."

But it wasn't a couple days; it was only a day and a half. Just as Corbin stepped out of the shower, his phone rang.

When Corbin answered, Hatch asked, "Are you ready?"

"Yeah, sure I am. Where am I going?"

"You're staying in England after all. A nice local job they want cleaned up fast. Seems Jonas is busy, so, with any luck, you won't even see him."

"So MI6 knows I'm here, with an active case, and will

leave me alone? I'll believe it when I see it. So what's the case?"

"We're not exactly sure yet, but a woman and two children have been kidnapped. They've been gone for two weeks, and now another woman with two children was kidnapped as well."

"I'm sure MI6 doesn't want me involved in that."

"Maybe not, but, as of now, a third woman has been taken—at least that's the ones we know of. We Mavericks wouldn't normally be involved with something like this either, but as we're on their turf ..."

"Well, *great*," Corbin noted. "Does this third woman have kids too?"

"No," Hatch replied. "However, she *is* pregnant."

"How on earth is that a good deal, ... even for a kidnapper?"

"It isn't, and the body of the first mother just showed up, and unfortunately her kids remain missing."

"Shit." Corbin's heart sank. "You know how I feel about kids."

"I know it, and, if you want to pass on this one, just tell me."

"No, I'm not passing on anything," he snapped. "I'll go in there. I can't stand any rat bastard who preys on kids. I'll take him down. Don't you worry."

"Oh, I believe you will." Hatch laughed. "Say hi to Nellie for me."

"Who is Nellie?" Corbin asked suspiciously.

"The daughter of one of the members of parliament. She's the latest woman who's gone missing."

"And do you know her?"

"Nope," he replied. "But obviously it's your turn at saving the damsel in distress, so chances are she'll become a good friend during this investigation. In which case I'll say hi in advance."

Corbin laughed. "Oh, Jesus, that's all I need. Well, I'll believe it when I see it. You look after Millie while I'm gone."

"Count on it," Hatch said quietly. "And you watch your back. I don't like that I won't be there to watch it for you. You will have a partner though. He's on his way, but, considering he's stateside, he'll be a day or two getting here, I understand."

And, with that, Corbin hung up and turned to pack. He knew this op would be hard, given the kids' element. It also needed to go down fast, and he needed to do it right. But, as always, he was ready.

"Well, Nellie, for better or for worse, here I come."

CHAPTER 1

CORBIN WALLACE STUDIED the area around him. He referred to his notes, double-checked the location, and realized this really was where Mary Hennessy and her two children were snatched in the first place—an unassuming corner in a small town, near the bus stop. It looked like she had been prepared to get on or to get off a bus with the kids. Possibly had changed her mind and accepted a ride from a deceptive friend or a friendly stranger. However, without eyewitnesses or security cameras, it was all conjecture.

But, from that point on, nobody knew what happened to her. It's as if she just vanished into thin air. Except her body had shown up in an industrial section, just outside of Heathrow Airport. No sign of her kids.

The fact that the children weren't with her was both good and bad itself. That no child-size bodies had shown up was great. What Corbin didn't know was whether the children were being moved or trafficked into the sex trade or maybe into illegal adoptions. He had no information at this point in time. *Nothing*. For all he knew, a woman who couldn't have children picked them up, deciding she wanted these two as her own family, killing the mother to get her out of the way.

It was a sick thought, but it was way better than the other options. What Corbin had now was a problem with further missing victims—a second mother and her two children and, on top of that, now the parliament member's daughter.

Corbin still wondered why the Mavericks had been called in on that last missing woman. He surmised that the parliament member was pulling any strings to get someone on his daughter's case. Corbin knew, if that were his daughter who had been taken, he'd want the Mavericks on the case, not MI6. Not that MI6 couldn't get the job done, but the Mavericks would be faster, less hindered.

Also apparently, Nellie Abrahms, the parliament member's daughter, was five months' pregnant. Which lent itself to all kinds of possibilities and one big ugly connection—children.

With a last look around at the empty bus stop, the empty road, and the rolling fields on both sides, Corbin hopped back into his vehicle and moved quickly to follow up where Mary Hennessy's body had been found.

According to the police reports that he'd gotten from Hatch, Hennessy died from a single bullet to the back of the head in an execution-style killing. The kidnappers-turned-murderers had made no contact with her family, had made no ransom demands or anything similar. So the kidnappers only wanted the kids, leaving their mother as extra baggage to be disposed of?

If so, Corbin had two other women who were in danger of meeting the same fate.

As soon as he arrived at the new GPS location, he noted it wasn't so much a construction site as it was a largely ignored property, out of the way from traffic, with piles of gravel off to one side and a couple old pieces of machinery on another. Also large stands of trees framed the other two sides. A perfect dump site. And one likely only known to locals.

Corbin wandered the open area to confirm if any security setup of any kind was installed here. Nope, not that he saw, and he knew where to look for evidence of same. Anybody could have driven up at any point in time to dump the body and then drive off without being seen. No street cameras. No businesses or homes in sight. So likely no help from anyone in the form of potential witnesses.

He found a lot of vehicle tracks, probably after the police had come to claim the body. Corbin shook his head at that, checked out the crime scene photos on his phone, and realized that she'd literally just been dropped on the ground, and then somebody had driven off.

His heart went out to the poor woman. Had she fought over her kids? Had she fought her attackers? Had she just been uncooperative or cranky, and her kidnappers decided she was too much trouble? Maybe she'd done her job and given birth to those two kids and caused trouble afterward, so got the ultimate trouble in return.

Hatch was doing a deep dive into her history to see whether she had any enemies, ex-husbands, or connection to the other two missing women.

With that in mind, he headed to where the second woman had been kidnapped—the parking lot of a grocery store. Apparently she'd been out very early in the morning and had been waiting for the store to open, according to one of the store's employees, who saw her waiting earlier in her car. In his eyewitness's account, he saw the car later, only nobody was in it.

When they realized that the vehicle was still there by the end of the business day, they called the police, which meant a whole twelve hours of time had been lost. She was a single, vulnerable, had no husband.

Shaking his head at that, Corbin went to the third site, where Nellie had been last seen. And that was the university where she was getting her master's degree. He wanted the campus's cooperation to check up on the cameras all over the place, but he knew the local cops had already checked and had confirmed no sign of her—other than at one o'clock on the day she went missing. That's apparently when she had headed outside, according to her friends, to meet somebody for lunch.

She hadn't been seen since. Did the authorities know for sure that she was with the same kidnappers? No. It was well-known that she was pregnant, trying to complete her degree before her delivery date. She was excited about the pregnancy, and it was not a case of giving up the baby for adoption or an unwanted pregnancy. However, no father was involved in the picture.

And that could be a completely different tangent to explore as well. What if the father wanted to be involved and had been cut out? Or what if he didn't want her to carry the child full-term? Corbin quickly sent a message to Hatch, asking him to check on that. When he got a thumbs-up back, he realized that the team was on it and that they were going over these concepts, as he was.

He slowly retraced his steps and headed to the residence of the first family. No crime scene tape was up, and the door was locked. He made his way in the back door of a small townhome. As he stepped inside, he found the place had been trashed. He stood here for a long moment, his hands in the pockets of his jeans, while he contemplated that scenario. Why trash the place, if they'd already picked up the woman and children? What did the kidnappers gain by that?

According to the police reports, the grandmother had gone through the place and couldn't see anything missing. The updates mentioned that the family hadn't been here in several months, so didn't really give any motive for a break-in later, unless someone knew the place was deserted and was looking for an easy score.

As Corbin wandered through the kids' rooms, he was looking for clothing, toys, anything that would help calm the children. He found no stuffed animals on either bed, but he didn't know if there ever had been. That was a question for the grandmother.

He checked the closets. They were stuffed so full that it would be almost impossible to see if something in particular had been removed from them. Then he headed to the mother's room. It had a double bed, neatly made, and her closet was painfully thin, compared to the kids. He realized that was the symbol of single motherhood, all over again. She had done what she needed to do for the children, but it was much harder to get what she needed for herself.

Shaking his head, he went back to the living room. Couches were tossed. Bookshelves were bare. Toys were in the middle of the floor. At that, he stopped and frowned because, of course, in many cases, families didn't put away playthings. So it's possible the toys mess had been here before the ransacking. But it still didn't make sense as to what the intruder was searching for—unless they took toys for the children and still left behind many more.

At the second residence, Corbin found a similar thing. Maybe not as badly torn apart as the first one, and that made him suspicious as to whether that was potentially just for show. Although what the ransacker thought that would do in terms of the investigation, Corbin had no idea.

But people thought very strange things when they were trying to throw law enforcement off their tracks and hide what they were actually up to. Corbin had hoped something here would tell him where to go next. And yet he saw nothing at either of the residences.

What he also found, as he walked through the second house, was no computer, no laptop, no electronic devices at all. Had the guys who'd kidnapped them stolen those items? Had the cops taken them? Or had just another thief after the fact taken advantage of the place being left empty with these easily sold items? Cases like this were probably all over the news, Corbin imagined, alerting the local riffraff. It wouldn't be much of a jump. And it wouldn't help his case either.

Unless … maybe the kidnappers were looking for medical records on the kids, for birth certificates even? That made some sense, along with getting the kids some familiar toys to keep them more settled during an otherwise unsettling time.

He quickly sent Hatch a couple questions on these new threads and carried on. As he drove up to Nellie's address, he noted a whole different story, and he highly doubted her place had been trashed. He held up his ID at the doorman, who just frowned at him, and Corbin walked on through to Nellie's apartment. This was a high-end section of town, classier and more secure than the two mothers' apartments that Corbin had just visited.

He knew he'd already been given the green light to search by MI6, but it was always a bit of a shit show to see who would call for enforcement regardless. He quickly used his own access and slipped inside her apartment. Once here, he noted the place was neat and untouched.

The baby's room was already prepped and ready, and—

according to the colors on the wall, green with a hint of yellow contrast—he presumed she didn't know the gender of the child she was expecting. He wandered through, looked at everything, and realized once again, *he found no laptop, no computer, nothing in terms of electronics and communications.* But then, if she'd been taken at the university, she likely had her laptop with her at the very time she had been kidnapped.

Shaking his head at that, he headed over to her desk. It was locked. He picked the lock and pulled open several drawers. He knew that the local cops had already been through this place, but that wasn't necessarily a help when he would assess things differently. Frowning, not liking the way the investigation was going so far, he quickly moved through the desk drawers, but not a whole lot was here.

When his phone rang a few minutes later, it was Hatch. "The parliament member is looking for progress."

"That would be nice. I've just gone through the three homes of the three known victims, and I'm currently at Nellie's apartment."

"Anything?"

"Nothing, as in scarily nothing."

"That's not good." Hatch swore. "Professional?"

"Professional at something. I'm still not sure that we have the same kidnapper for all three."

"But Nellie was pregnant."

"Which is a big difference than having two kids." He stood, looked around Nellie's high-end apartment. "So either we have different kidnappers here or the kidnappers have evolved their game."

"I get it. It's not some premise we can knock off, but I'm not sure that it's anything that we can lock down either." A long pause came, then Hatch asked, "Next move?"

"I'm heading back to the university to find her friends. Did we have a list?"

"We have very few. Just from what we know now, she was friendly with everyone but only had a rare couple of best friends, people who really got to know Nellie. I can send them to you."

"That'd be good. I want to talk to them and see whether she had anybody in her life recently or the father of her child was around. Plus I want to ensure her laptop was with her at the time she went missing. I found no laptops or computers at the previous residences."

"According to everything that the police reported, Nellie never told anybody who the father was."

"Sure, but, depending on who she was as a person, and her stature in reference to the baby's father and/or her own father, one of those fathers may have just found out himself that she was pregnant. And might have been unimpressed."

"Yeah, the parliament member certainly is," Hatch said cautiously, "but that's not enough to go on."

"It's not enough for anything possible yet," Corbin murmured, "but it is enough to start the wheels turning. I need the contact information of the grandmothers in the first two cases and that list of Nellie's friends, anyone who may have known her movements leading up to this—like where she was, where she could have gone, things like that."

"It's all in the file," Hatch noted cheerfully.

"The file is really thin," Corbin snapped.

"I know," Hatch replied, his voice lowering. "In Mary's case, she didn't have much in the way of friends. She was living on social security benefits and was figuring out what to do with her life apparently. I suspect she didn't have a laptop, using her phone for everything."

"Right. While she was doing that introspection, raising those kids would have been her priority."

"It was evident that she was a devoted mother, and somebody noticed. The kids have been to the doctors a couple times over their young lives but no red flags. They weren't school age yet, so no public records there."

"Okay, have the team continue to hunt down answers for me, and I'm heading to the university."

With that, Corbin hung up on Hatch and headed back to the university. By going to Nellie's dean's office, he accessed the schedules for Nellie's student friends. With that out of the way, he quickly contacted several of them on the phone. Two people answered, both female, and—when he explained what he was doing and what he needed—he arranged for them to meet. Both agreed.

Setting the interviews at forty-five minutes apart, he met them outside the cafeteria, where he sat with them for a cup of coffee. When he watched one woman approach—Carly, his first interview—looking around nervously, he quickly got up and identified himself.

She nodded and sat down beside him. "I need to see some ID."

"Good enough." And he held out his ID.

She studied it, nodded. "I don't understand."

"What's to understand?" he asked, frowning. "Your friend is missing."

"I know, but I thought the local police were looking into it."

"Her father has asked my department to look into it as well," he said quietly. "So I need to know everything about her."

Carly winced at that. "She wouldn't like that. She is a

very private person."

"Maybe normally she would mind, but not if she's in trouble, right? Her privacy won't matter as much, if she needs help."

Her friend's shoulders sagged, and she nodded. "Nellie and her father didn't get along particularly well, since the pregnancy ..."

"He didn't want her to keep the baby?"

"He was mad that she wouldn't tell him who the father was."

"Ah, well, that's definitely an issue too."

"She had a couple long-term relationships, and her father blew them up, both of them. Nellie figured that, at this point in time, her father would always interfere in her life, so she tried to cut him out, but it wasn't working."

"Fathers have a tendency to get a little heavy-handed." She eyed him sideways, and he shrugged. "And obviously, in this case, it was too heavy-handed."

"You don't understand," she whispered.

"No, I don't, but it would be nice if I had an idea of what was going on."

"She wanted to disappear. Nellie wanted to have the baby, without her father hassling her or coming by the hospital and telling her again to abort or at the very least give it up for adoption."

"I doubt adoption was on her mind."

"Well, she thought about it, but only when she was majorly depressed and usually because of her father."

At that, Corbin studied her. "Is there something I need to know about her relationship with her father?"

"Only that it was always fraught with difficulty," she murmured, "and I know for a fact that he didn't want her to have anything to do with keeping this child."

"She must have figured that her father would never ease up. So she decided to go ahead and have it anyway?"

Carly nodded at that. "That was my take on it, but we didn't really talk about it. I did ask her if she was scared about doing this alone, and she said yes, but she was also determined."

"Right, because anything else would be too hard to live with."

She looked over at him in surprise. "You do understand."

"I understand human nature," he murmured.

"She's a really nice person. I hope everything is okay."

"Do you think she's really missing, or do you think she's just disappeared to be on her own?" At that, he got a flat stare.

"I don't know. I would have hoped that, if she had decided to disappear, she would say something to me."

"And I guess that's the question that I'm coming to right now." He stared at his first witness intently, but she didn't flinch. "I'm afraid something's seriously wrong. I know the police are very concerned, but they're also toeing Daddy's line. She's been reported missing, so, therefore, as far as the police are concerned, it's a big deal on its own. However, we also have several other cases of missing women."

"Of course you do." She shrugged and stared at a spot behind his shoulder. "Hey, it's not like people don't go missing nearly every day. The public thinks it won't happen to them. Plus I think Nellie was totally focused on having this baby and avoiding her father."

"Safety is an interesting thing. It's not always what it appears to be."

"You know what? *That's* something she would agree with. She would totally say that safety was an internal thing and that she wouldn't ever really feel safe again."

"Did something happen to her before? Something that triggered this reaction in her, so that she didn't feel safe?" he asked quietly.

"Yes, absolutely. It was another kidnapping attempt from quite a few years ago, and I think it's also why her father is so protective."

He pulled up Nellie's file on his phone. "I don't have any listing of any such prior incident."

"Not too many people even know about it. It wasn't public knowledge."

"So what happened?"

"There was a kidnapping, about ten years ago maybe." She stopped, frowned. "It could have been even further back than that, maybe thirteen years ago."

"She would have been about sixteen?"

Her friend nodded. "Yeah, so would have been around then."

"What happened?"

"She woke up to an intruder in the house. He had a gun and forced her out of the home, where he walked her down the block to his vehicle. He tried to get her into his vehicle, and she fought back. As soon as she started screaming, making a ruckus, rather than shooting her, he hopped into the front seat of the vehicle and took off."

"Interesting. That should be in her file."

"No, I think her dad squashed it pretty good," she said, with a wry look. "After that, everything became even more impossible. Nellie felt smothered constantly. And every time she had a boyfriend, her dad would tear apart his life. He had a knack of finding something and then used it to force the guy away."

"So her father is very controlling."

"But he also came close to losing her so …"

"Got it," he murmured. "Sounds like I need to have a follow-up with dear old dad."

"I highly doubt that this old event is related to her disappearance."

"Maybe, but it's also possible she has taken off on her own, rather than letting her dad in on her life."

"Yes, you're right." She stared at him pensively. "Nellie should have at least let somebody know, so that we could tell the family that she's just choosing to not see anybody."

Privately Corbin thought the whole thing was a nightmare, but people, especially when threatened, acted unpredictably. And when hormones were added into the mix and a pregnancy …

NELLIE ABRAHMS OPENED her eyes and then slammed them shut again. "How many times do I have to do this?" she whispered. "It's a never-ending nightmare."

A snicker came from beside her. "Hey. It'll still be the same when you wake up in a day or two. It is all your life is now."

"Does it ever change?" she asked quietly, her eyes still closed.

"Yeah, when they come," the other woman whispered, dread in her voice. "You don't want that."

"No, I really don't." Nellie's hands protectively cradled her pregnant belly. "Are you pregnant too?" she asked, her worst nightmare leading with the questions.

"No," she hesitated, then reluctantly added, "I have a one-year-old."

"With you?" she asked in horror.

"Yes," she whispered, but such defeat filled her voice. "She's in another room. I get to see her every once in a while—if I'm good."

"Dear God."

"I know, and, before you ask, I don't know what they're doing with us. I don't know why they want us. I don't know what they're doing with my daughter. But she appears to be happy, outside of the fact that she can't see me anytime she wants to, but she's doing okay." Her voice broke at the end of that sentence.

"Well, that's something," Nellie said in a hoarse whisper.

"It is, but it's not enough."

"Of course not." Nellie shifted onto her elbows to look around the small room, empty but for the two beds. "I would really like to know what the hell they're planning for us here." She studied the other woman in the gloomy light. "Is it just you and me?"

"No, two more women are one room down."

When her roommate fell silent, Nellie felt compelled to keep asking, "Are they okay?"

"From the sounds I hear, they fight with the guards every time."

"Then what?"

"Then they get beaten up," the woman snapped. "I can't get close to them to tell them to stop, but I don't even know if those two women realize anybody else is here. I think the two of them are pretty panicked."

"That makes sense then, doesn't it?"

"It does, but it would be nice if we could let them know that we're here too, that they are not alone."

"Have they got they're children too?"

"I would presume so. There are other kids who play with my daughter all the time."

"They're okay with that?"

"I think it's a punishment for them. The mothers can't see their kids, if the mothers don't behave."

"Well, I would behave immediately," Nellie whispered.

"Yeah, but these two have had a little more fighting spirit, and maybe … I don't know." She stopped speaking for a moment, then reluctantly added, "I think it's too easy to judge."

"What about any others?"

First came silence. "There was one more."

"And what happened to her?"

"She's dead."

"Oh, no." Nellie bolted into a sitting position to stare at the only door in terror. "Oh, God, will that happen to us?"

"Well, we can hope not." The other woman glared at her. "It's a hell of a way to keep us in line."

"Yet it's not keeping the other two mothers in line."

"I'm not sure that they know about it yet. Although the sounds were hard to miss, considering she was killed here."

"Shit. How?"

"They put a bullet in her."

"Do you know why?"

"Yeah, sure I do. She fought back and almost took them out. They decided that she was way too much trouble. Believe me. They told me all about it."

"Please don't tell me that she had kids too."

"I presume they each have two because I count six other

kids with mine."

"Jesus. Do any of the kids ask for their mothers?"

"No, at least I've never heard them."

"Maybe they don't think their mothers are here any-more."

"I hope they didn't see the one die," the other woman whispered. "That would be my wish."

"Can you tell me how long you've been here?"

"A couple months now."

"Jesus, and you still don't know what they want?"

"They want our kids," the other woman said quietly. "And, as much as you'll say they can't have yours, I'm telling you that ... you might as well get used to it. Because they have no intention of letting you leave *with* your baby. Chances are good that you won't leave at all."

CHAPTER 2

NELLIE CURLED UP in a ball, her hands hugging her belly, as she thought about everything the other woman had said. She'd fallen quiet and since then hadn't answered any whispered questions. Nellie didn't know whether her roommate was sleeping or just keeping silent, but her breathing was slow and even.

They were now in complete darkness, and it appeared to be some underground room, as far as Nellie could tell. Underground may not be likely, but there were no visible windows, or maybe something covered the windows. What she didn't know was what this was all about. Or why it was happening in the first place.

If she hadn't been so pigheaded about keeping her father out of her life—and his private security detail—someone would know that Nellie was missing. But she made a point of telling even her friends about her aversion toward her father's methods and her wish to be strictly on her own. They quite possibly thought she'd left on her own.

Right now, she just wanted to know someone was looking for her. Maybe even her father. She knew how angry her father was about her pregnancy and how absolutely unimpressed he was that she was planning on raising this child on her own. He was incensed that she wouldn't even tell him who the father was. ... That was an explosive situation. But, all their differences aside, she knew he loved her, in his own controlling way.

So why the hell had it taken until now to realize that? She could have put her foot down, somewhere along the line, and made him understand her point of view. She clearly had had plenty of chances. She just hadn't addressed the problem. Instead, rather than have that conflict, she had avoided it. And now look where the hell she was?

She ran her hand over her face, wondering how she would get out of this. She wasn't somebody who got into trouble, but wow. ... She'd done it this time. *What a nightmare.*

She rocked herself slowly to sleep, waking with bits and pieces of the nightmare coming back to her over and over again. She'd been walking along the campus, heading toward home, when two men came up on either side of her, had thrown a bag over her head. Before she'd had a chance to react, she'd been picked up and tossed into the back of a vehicle. Then there was a period of blackout. Since waking up here, Nellie had been supplied with only food and water, and that was it.

She didn't even know how many days had gone by. She woke at the sound of the door opening. Immediately she scrambled upright on the bed and pulled up against the headboard. The room was dim, and she could only make out a hulking shape.

"Good, you're awake," said the man from the gloom.

She nodded slowly. "I am," she murmured cautiously. "What do you want with me?" Only silence came. "May I go to the bathroom?"

"Ah, yes, nothing like pregnant bellies for bladder control." He laughed. "Sure, come on." And he reached out a hand and grabbed her by the arm and squeezed. "If you try anything? … Believe me. It won't go well for you." She didn't say anything but let him lead her into a small room, dimly lit. Still the light cheered her.

He left the door open and said, "Go ahead."

She realized that he had no intention of shutting the door. She cast him a sideways glance, but her bladder really was full.

He shook his head. "I couldn't give a shit about raping you," he snapped, with a sarcastic look. "Basketball bellies do not appeal to me, so do your thing."

For that, she could be grateful. At five months along, she was definitely getting a baby belly. She walked over to the toilet—thankfully hidden behind a partition wall, without a door—and quickly relieved herself. The small room had peeling gray paint, yet was surprisingly clean. At the tiny sink, she washed her hands. She looked around for a towel to dry her hands, but none were anywhere in sight. She stepped out into the main part of the bathroom, hating to leave the comfort of the light, when he looked up and nodded.

"Get back to your bed and lay down again."

The bathroom was attached to the same bedroom, and the light gave her a chance to glance around, trying to lock the images of where they were in her mind, before she had to lay down and knew that he would take away the light. Nellie saw two beds, an empty one—hers—and the second bed with a woman—maybe the roommate Nellie had spoken to earlier. The other woman didn't appear to be doing so good. "Is she all right?" Nellie asked anxiously.

He nodded. "She will be. Unless she pulls any more stupid stunts."

Nellie wasn't even sure what that meant because, as far

as she understood, this woman had been cooperating. Nellie sat down cautiously on her bed, wincing as the baby gave her a kick.

He saw the wince and smiled. "So now you'll start whining and say you need more pillows or comforters or something, right?"

"No, not that, ... only that I could really use some food."

"Food is coming," he said, looking at her. "Good thing you're not wasting my time."

"How would I waste it?" she murmured.

"By asking stupid questions."

Hearing his words, immediately all Nellie's questions died on her tongue. Especially if asking them would only piss him off. She wanted to ask a ton of questions, but, if he wouldn't be cooperative, there was no point.

And, with that, he walked out again. But he'd left the bathroom light on, and, for that, she was grateful.

She glanced around the room, trying to memorize what was here. One door in and out. She didn't know if it was locked, as she hadn't heard a *click*. It was probably a test to see if she would run out after him, but there was absolutely no point. Nellie wasn't in any shape, either to run or to even walk right now. And that was something that concerned her in a really big way. She needed food and rest. She was normally in great health and fit, but she was still five months' pregnant and showing more than she'd expected.

But what did she know? She lay back down on the bed. There was a single blanket that she pulled up over the top of her shoulders. The room wasn't cold, but there was a chill inside Nellie that she found hard to argue with.

Pulling her knees up, she rolled on her side and waited.

And waited. Her eyes drifted closed. When she opened them the next time, a man stood in front of her. She jolted but managed to hold back a scream.

"Good. Hopefully you'll be one who doesn't give me trouble."

"It's not my plan," she whispered, and she noted he held out a plate of food. She reached for the plate and smiled. "Thank you." She looked around, hoping for a drink.

He frowned and snapped, "Now what?"

She hated to ask, but her throat was dry. "Water?"

"Oh, right. I forgot to pick that up." He disappeared out the same door. Again he didn't lock it and popped back in again a few minutes later, with a bottle of water. He threw it onto her bed and disappeared.

She wasn't exactly sure why she was getting this treatment. The other woman appeared to be unconscious. Nellie put down her plate and walked over to check whether her roommate was sleeping or dead. She looked peaceful, but she was not showing any signs of waking. Nellie figured it was much more of a drug-induced sleep.

Shuddering at the thought, she sat down again and ate slowly. It was pretty tasteless, but it was food, and she was not in a position to argue, especially if this guy was weeding out people who were causing him trouble. Something bad could get really ugly, if she didn't choose the right path. So, for the moment, the path of least resistance was exactly where she would go. What she really needed was somebody to come riding to the rescue.

An hour later she was woken from a light doze. Her guard tossed a sheet of paper on the bed in front of her. She picked it up and looked at it—a picture of a man—then looked at her guard. "Who's this guy?"

"We're not sure," he replied, eyeing her closely. "Do you know him?"

She looked at the black-and-white features again, but it was hard to see the image in the poor light. She shook her head. "No. I don't think I've ever seen him before."

"Take a good look," he ordered.

Surprised, she looked at it again, then asked, "May I take it to the light?" He nodded. She got up, went to the bathroom, and held it under the lighting there, and then shook her head. "No, I don't know him."

"Well, he's looking for you. He's been talking to your friends and family members."

She frowned, then shrugged. "I don't know anything about him."

"Apparently his name is Corbin, and he works for a special arm of the US military."

She stared at him in shock. "*US* military?"

"Yes." He narrowed his gaze, as if looking for a lie. "That's why we're concerned."

She nodded. "Honestly I've never seen him before. I don't know his features, and I don't know anyone in the US."

"Well, we know about your daddy and did expect him to hire somebody eventually."

"Right. I don't know if you're after ransom money, but Daddy has it."

"Makes sense but this isn't a simple kidnapping case."

She nodded. "Okay," she said quietly. She put the photo on her bed. Something was oddly familiar about him. Yet she didn't know why. "I don't know him," she repeated.

He nodded. "Good enough for now." And, with that, he turned and left.

She wanted to ask about the other women but didn't. Nellie turned to look at her roommate, only the second bed was empty.

Had the woman left while Nellie slept? She frowned at that because she didn't want to think that she'd been out so long. Had they drugged her food? That was even more upsetting because of the baby. That shouldn't be done at all but definitely not while pregnant.

As she lay here, she realized the baby wasn't moving at all. She started to massage her belly and whispered to her child, "It's okay, baby. It's okay. We'll get out of this." Within minutes, her baby moved, and Nellie gave a big sigh of relief. "I haven't even met you yet, and I have never loved someone more. We'll get out of this. I promise you."

And, of course with that thought, her mind returned to the stranger in the photo. "Corbin ..." What kind of a name was that anyway? She had no doubt it was somebody her father had hired. Which made her feel better to know someone was looking for her. But was it somebody good? And what if her father hadn't hired him? It didn't matter. Someone was looking for her.

Feeling better, she snuggled under the blanket, whispering to him, "Well, Corbin, I don't know who you are or why you're looking for me, but please find me and my baby soon, damn it."

NEXT CORBIN MET with the second university student, Louise, who was supposedly a good and close friend of Nellie's. His first interview had gone longer than expected, and Corbin didn't want these two witnesses to be aware of each other. It was as much to protect his own investigation, to not taint any testimony, as well as to not put these students in the kidnappers' crosshairs. While both students were friends of Nellie's, it had not yet been confirmed that both students knew each other as well. So Corbin was playing it safe.

He breathed a sigh of relief when Carly left just one minute before Louise appeared. They exchanged greetings, and Corbin asked if she would like a coffee. She nodded, sat down, and Corbin got himself another cup, as he placed her order. Soon he was seated with his next informant. "How did you know Nellie?" he asked her.

Louise swallowed, her hands nervous, as she gazed about her surroundings. "Will I get kidnapped if I talk to you about Nellie getting kidnapped?"

Corbin frowned. "I can put a tail on you, if that would make you feel better, feel safer." He waited for her reply. She was breathing faster now. Corbin waited her out.

With one more glance over her shoulder, she nodded. It was a discreet nod.

"Will do." He immediately sent a text to Hatch, to put someone on this young lady. He smiled when he got confirmation. "Done. He will show up before we are through talking, so he sees you with me and knows you're the one he needs to protect."

"Thank you," Louise whispered.

"No problem," Corbin replied. "This is what we do. Can you tell me what has you so spooked?"

She stared at him, as if the question itself were insane.

"What I'm asking is, has someone threatened you, whether in person or via a text or just a note on your dorm room door?

Her hand immediately went to her chest. "God, no. Is that what will happen if I speak to you further?"

"No. That's why my man is coming. Remember?"

Louise sighed loudly. "Right. Right."

"So have you been threatened?"

She shook her head. "No. But you must understand how, if a parliament member's own daughter can be kidnapped from a well-known university in broad daylight, it could upset a lot of female students here."

Corbin nodded. "I understand. However, both the university police and the local police have been alerted, as has my independent team. Believe me. The university officials don't want a repeat of this. They are helping me with my investigation as much as possible. Plus the parliament member is making sure the university is on high alert, watching out for the rest of you." Finally that hand on her chest slowly fell to her lap.

And their coffees were delivered to them.

Corbin was thankful for that timely arrival as well. Now maybe he could actually ask his questions and get some answers from Louise. "So how did you know Nellie?"

She took a sip of her coffee and nodded. "My father was a parliament member at one time as well. I remember the security around me all the time—although I was a child back then, so maybe that recollection is wrong. However, Nellie's father knew my father, and so I was introduced to Nellie as a child. We've never been really close, until now. Until we both started uni here. In fact, we were roommates for a while, living on campus—until she was pregnant and wanted to live on her own."

"So what do you know of her boyfriend, the father of her child?"

Louise shook her head, frowning. "I was shocked that she was pregnant because I didn't even know she was seeing anyone."

"So," Corbin began, "was Nellie always this secretive about her boyfriends?"

"No, not at all. At least, not with me and her closest friends. She was always honest and upfront with us. We knew all about the last two men she dated and how her father broke them up each time. Which is why I'm kinda mad at her for not letting me know more of what was going on in her life currently. Although … I knew her father. *Overprotective* doesn't begin to explain him."

"Three things. I need a list of her close friends, and I want to know more about her father, but, right now, what about those two old boyfriends? Tell me more about them."

"Like what?"

"Names, where they are now?"

"The last one—that *I* knew about—was Ali Ewing. Believe it or not he decided to be a priest and is off studying for his bachelor's degree somewhere so he can be ordained. … I can't remember where or the name of the university."

"Not to worry. I'll get my team on it." Corbin promptly texted the info to Hatch so that the team could get on it. "And the other recent beau?"

"I'm trying to remember his name. He got caught cheating on an exam and was expelled from uni."

"Here?" Corbin asked.

"Yes."

"Maybe the dean can help me with that."

"Good." Louise frowned. "I can't remember his name at all. It might come to me later."

Corbin slid one of his cards over to her. "Call me if you

remember *anything*. So, if he's no longer here, do you know what he's been up to lately?"

"I think he was in jail soon after he was expelled. Of course his family was livid and cut him off. So maybe he was stealing food or something? Again, I'm sorry. I just don't remember any details."

Corbin busily texted Hatch again to find this elusive ex-boyfriend. "Was Nellie known to date people like this guy?"

"Like cheaters, thieves?" she asked. He nodded. "No. No, not at all. She's a straight arrow and wanted someone whose beliefs aligned with hers."

"So dating a married man would be out of the question with Nellie?" he asked, suddenly very interested in the answer and not for purposes of this op.

"No way." Louise shook her head vehemently. "You've got to understand what it's like being a parliament member's kid. The paparazzi are always around to catch you doing the least little thing, turning it into a big scandal in the gossip rags. Our dads had *the talk* with us about not embarrassing them in the press. Being teenagers, now adults with a sex life, can both be hard on the public faces of the parliament members."

Corbin almost chuckled at her grimace. "So now's a good time to talk about her father."

Louise took another sip of her coffee, then sighed. "I know probably every kid, of any age, has had conflicts with their parents at times. But, speaking from personal experience, they don't have it as bad as parliament member kids do—unless their parents are some celebrities, like actors or royalty or such." She shook her head. "So comparing my father to hers? I'm just so glad I got mine and not Nellie's. He was paranoid."

"Paranoid, how?"

"When we were kids, having sleepovers, she came with a whole security detail. My dad may have had one or two on me at the same time, but they were pretty nice about it, staying in the background. No way with Nellie's dad. He told my dad that Nellie would not attend any overnight stays unless he had a man inside, plus the team outside, as well as full access to my dad's security, both physical and digital."

"Do you know why he was so paranoid?"

Louise went on to tell him about the earlier kidnapping event that Carly had spoken of not an hour before.

Corbin sent off another quick text to Hatch. "Anything else?"

Louise cocked her head, narrowed her eyes, as if considering something. "Seems like there was an earlier incident ..."

"Before she was almost kidnapped at age sixteen?" That had him sitting up straighter.

Louise began to nod slowly. "I think it was a ... fire." She shook her head at Corbin. "Sorry. That was so long ago that I'm fuzzy on this recollection."

"Does Nellie remember it, to your knowledge?"

"Oh, yes. It was something that set her dad off for sure, but—and I know this will sound weird—she seemed to have fond memories of it."

Corbin's eyebrows went up. "Can you explain that?"

"Nope. Never knew why. Always thought it odd. But, now that I think of it, she was secretive way back then." She slumped in her chair. "Wow. Maybe she's been that way for much longer than I had imagined."

"But you understood why she had to distance herself from her dad, right?"

"Oh, yeah. The man was relentless. Dogging her to get an abortion. Even now at five months' pregnant. Demanding Nellie tell him the name of the baby's father. He threatened to cut her uni funding, but Nellie called his bluff, started distancing herself from him more and more. And that just made him more fanatical. He called me more than a few times, *questioning* me." She shivered at the thought.

"Like I am doing?" Corbin asked, to get a reading off her.

"Not even close," she spat. "Even after I changed my phone number, *twice*, he still called me. If he had been my father, I would have disowned him long ago. Yet ... Nellie may lay down rules and boundaries with her dad, but she's still got a soft spot for him. I just don't get it. He's horrid to her. If that's what he sees as love, I don't want anything to do with it."

"What about other family in Nellie's life?"

Louise grimaced. "She lost her mom early on. Which kinda explains the overprotective dad issue, I guess. And he never remarried. *Huh.* Maybe he couldn't handle the pain of losing someone else?" With that thought, she faced Corbin. "Do you think that's what has been going on with him?"

"Could very well explain it."

"*Hmm.* Maybe I should not be so hard on him."

"So Nellie has no siblings or aunts or uncles or grandparents or such? Any other close friends you know of?"

She frowned. "That's so weird. I knew of our mutual friends, back when we were younger. Now I don't know of another friend of hers. *Wow.* Nellie has been keeping some secrets. As to your question about family, I know of no close relatives, that's for sure. It's pretty much been just Nellie and her dad for probably ... two decades maybe? Oh my God, I didn't think of that either. Not in the context of her hovering dad or even from Nellie's perspective. I haven't been such a good friend if I didn't notice all that in her life until now, have I?"

Corbin could tell she was looking for some reassurance. "You can't go back and fix anything, but you can change things going forward."

She gasped. "*If* she comes back …"

"I'll find her," Corbin promised. Of course he didn't promise that he would find Nellie alive, although that was his intention. By now Louise was distraught, and Corbin nodded to the man in jeans with a ball cap, who stood alone but nearby. Corbin grabbed one of Louise's hands to hold her attention. "Don't look now, but your tail is here."

He was surprised when she didn't reflexively take a glance. "What we'll do is, I'll stand, walk behind your chair, pull it out, then grab your hand again to turn you in the direction of the man in a blue baseball cap, so you won't be afraid if you see him around at times."

Louise nodded numbly.

Corbin got her up and turned her in the right direction. "You see him, right?"

She nodded, barely noting her tail, then dropping her gaze. "I'm not going to classes today. I need … to get myself together. Can you tell that man that I'm going to my dorm room?"

"Sure." Corbin texted the guy, but the tail didn't answer his phone, just giving Corbin a discrete chin-up signal. That way, anybody watching wouldn't see the tail immediately grabbing his phone, giving away his part in all this. Even as Louise walked with determination back to her dorm, the guy waited, turned away, then shortly meandered from her for a bit, stopping to talk to a student—probably asking for fake directions. He nodded, then course corrected toward Louise's building, which she had just entered, now out of sight.

CORBIN SAT INSIDE his vehicle, a cup of coffee in his hand, as he wrote down his longer notes from his interviews with both Carly and Louise, when Hatch rang. "We're working on your tips. I'll let you know when we have something. Meanwhile, the parliament member, Nellie's father, has received a warning to take you off the case."

He lifted his head and stared out the windshield. *Say what?* "Me? Off the case?"

"Yes, something you did pissed someone right off."

"Who?"

"Well, I'll say the kidnappers, but Nellie's dad has no answers as to who called. However, we're using all our tools and contacts to see if we can trace that call. Just some message about you needed to be reined back in again."

"Interesting." Corbin gave a feral smile. "I just got here and barely started my investigation, and I've already touched a thread that set off the bad guys. *Go figure.*"

"And it's been noted. Somebody saw you talking to somebody."

"Or somebody I talked to then spoke to somebody." His mind raced, going over the list of university officials and local authorities he'd spoken to—plus his latest two interviewees. None raised a red flag. *Must have spies on the ground.* "So what does Nellie's father want me to do?"

"He wants you to redouble your efforts because you're

pissing somebody off."

That was good. Corbin pissing someone off *could* be a good thing. "Even though it could get his daughter killed?"

"We all know how this works," Hatch said. "If you listen to the kidnappers, then they have the upper hand."

"They already have the upper hand anyway."

"I think, in this case, we can all agree that Nellie was kidnapped for her child. Since she's only five months along, I don't think even the kidnappers would induce birth this early. Regardless her father is hoping you'll find something fast, before they can harm his daughter. That you've already triggered this kind of reaction is a good thing."

"But did the local cops get the same warning? The uni police?"

"Not that I heard, but I'll double-check."

"Still," Corbin added, "what did the kidnappers think would happen when kidnapping a current parliament member's daughter? Surely they had vetted their potential victims to a certain extent. If not, this was really amateur hour. Plus I'm just thinking back to who would have talked—or who had been asked about Nellie and this investigation. I gotta say that I don't see any red flags, which just means the kidnappers have a man on the ground here."

"Good point. We figured that, but now we have confirmation," Hatch stated.

Almost immediately Corbin's mind went to the two student interviews he'd just conducted today, and they both mentioned one common theme. "Well, the threat answers one question. She was definitely kidnapped. Both of the students I'd talked to earlier today mentioned that the relationship between Nellie's father and Nellie was really bad. Carly figures that Nellie would have, in many ways, taken off, just so that her father wouldn't be a part of Nellie's life. But Carly also said that, if Nellie did take off, she would have let her friends know. Which is what most people would have expected. Which is what my second student interviewed, Louise, also noted. So now we know for sure that Nellie didn't disappear. She was taken."

"Did either student have any particular reasons why Nellie's father is so protective?"

"Yes," he snorted. "Apparently there was an attempted kidnapping of her from her childhood home, when she was sixteen. And that's after she was rescued from a fire at the age of ten."

"What?" Hatch snapped. "We have the fire noted in our files but have no mention of the earlier kidnapping attempt."

"I know. Makes me wonder what else good ol' dad has scrubbed from public data. Since then *Daddy* has been domineering, overprotective, and controlling. Maybe you should mention that to the parliament member the next time he calls. We need to know relevant intel like that."

"Will do. But that added data makes sense. If you come close to losing your daughter, wouldn't you want to make sure that she's safe ever after?"

"Yes, but apparently it's gotten to the point where he goes over every boyfriend's history, tearing apart his life and even that of his family, until the parliament member finds something that he can then destroy them with, so that they walk away and leave Nellie on her own."

"Nasty and not very good on her dad's part."

Corbin added, "Of course now that she's pregnant and that she won't tell him who the father is, he's beside himself."

"Of course he is because now he feels like he's failed, and

again he can't fix this because she's gone missing. Of course, even worse, he was trying to fix it beforehand. So, in many ways, it's a double whammy for him."

"Exactly."

Hatch asked Corbin, "Do you think the two students you spoke to may have had something to do with this warning?"

"Nope. I didn't get that from either of them."

"Okay. I'm just wondering if either of your interviewees told somebody else—and, if so, who and why?"

Immediately Corbin shook his head, even though he was on the phone with Hatch. "That implies Carly and/or Louise were part of the kidnapping event—or somebody one of them know is part of it and is sharing intel with the kidnappers. Yet these are two university students, who, while young and rich, have their heads on pretty straight. I don't see them for this."

"Had to ask. You know we're just tossing out straws at the moment? Do you have a list of everyone you've talked to so far?"

"Yes, I'll take a picture of it and send it through."

"And did you discuss the other cases?"

"Yes, but only with Louise, my second interviewee."

"Which just goes back to that theory that potentially they're not related." They pondered that, then Hatch added, "And how do you feel about it?"

"I have no reason to feel either way at the moment," Corbin said cautiously, "but it doesn't feel right to go in that *not related* direction. There's just such a connection between pregnancy and young children that it's not one I'm prepared to ignore."

"No, of course not. Anyway, watch your back. Especially

now that somebody knows you're here, looking into this."

"Got it." Corbin sighed. "More than that, their man on the ground will now know that I'm here looking and that I've been warned off too. So, if I don't stop, they will know Daddy won't play their game."

"Exactly," Hatch added. "We have to move fast and keep Nellie safe."

"Sure, but we first must find out where she is, so we can actually keep her safe."

"Get back to me as soon as you can."

"Yeah. I need the team to do a sweep of the security cameras on that university. I know the local authorities viewed it, maybe uni police too, but somebody took Nellie from that location. So, if she isn't showing up in any of the vehicles, then I want a list of all the vans that went through the place; and if work vehicles were seen there, I want to know what companies were possibly involved."

"We're on it," Hatch said, and, with that, he hung up.

Corbin stared down at his phone, wondering how the kidnappers already knew about him. Considering the fact that they were already warning him to keep off the case was alarming.

"Why me?" he wondered aloud. "The local cops were here. They had to have ruffled some feathers too. Plus lots of university officials were around, looking for her, so why me?"

And, of course, the easy answer was that the kidnappers had thought this investigation would die a quick death with the normal law enforcement process. So that failure brought in Corbin, a new face and an unknown element. And maybe the kidnappers were afraid that Corbin would find something.

Because that's really what it came down to. There was no

need to put out a warning, *unless* the kidnappers thought Corbin would find something. He planned to redouble his efforts.

For a long moment, he thought about the people he'd spoken to. But the one who really came to mind was the first student friend of Nellie's. "Carly had to know something more."

On that note he headed toward the main university campus. Somewhere along the line, she must have mentioned it to somebody. He wanted to know who. As soon as he got to the campus, he called her to see what class she was in.

She didn't answer, didn't pick up. With a foreboding instinct that told him something was seriously wrong, he pulled up her address and her class schedule and then quickly phoned Hatch. "See if Carly showed up this afternoon for her classes."

"What's wrong?" Hatch asked.

"My instincts are screaming at me. She's not answering her phone. I'm heading to her dorm."

"Will do."

And, with that, Corbin took off toward her residence. When he got to the right address, he stepped into the coed dormitory and headed for Carly's room straightaway. He knocked on the door, and, when he got no answer and heard no movement or other noise inside, he turned and looked around. A guy walked down the hall toward Corbin. "Hey, do you know the woman, Carly, who lives here?"

"Yeah, sure, but I haven't seen her today, if that's what you're asking."

"I spoke with her this morning," Corbin noted. And then he thought about it. "At least I think that was who I was talking to." He pulled out his phone and held up the picture of Carly. "Is that her?"

"Yes, that's her, and this is her place." He knocked on the door and called out, "Hey, Carly, are you in there?" But there was only silence. "She should be at classes anyway. You should check that first."

"Will do." Corbin waited for the guy to disappear, pulled out his tools, and quickly opened the door. His heart sinking, he closed the door and called Hatch immediately. "I'm inside her dorm."

"And?"

"It's the worst." He studied the woman on the floor. "Blunt force trauma at the back of the head. Door was locked, so somebody with a key. It is likely somebody she knows did this. She told him what she needed to tell him, whether it was by force or not, and then she was killed here."

"Damn. Cops are on their way. We'll tear apart her life."

"I don't want to be held up by talking to any cops right now, so I'm leaving."

With that, he stepped back out again, making sure nobody was around to see him, and quickly walked away. The university would be crawling with cops soon enough. And he didn't want to get caught in that cycle. Besides what he needed was the camera feed.

He quickly sent a text message to Hatch. **I need the camera feed from the university covering that dorm room over the last three hours.**

Got it. BTW, both previous boyfriends of Nellie are cleared. The one is in seminary in the States. Confirmed by the university's head office. The second turns out to be a career criminal and remains in jail. No visitors in the last year, so doesn't seem like any mastermind relevant to our time period.

41

And, with that update, Corbin returned to his truck. His day had been busy. He hadn't even had a chance to check in at his accommodations. Just then his phone buzzed. Hatch had sent him the security feeds from the university. When he checked his phone, the feed wasn't clear enough to see anything. Swearing, he quickly drove to the room that had been booked for him.

It was actually a small apartment, not too far away, which was good and yet also bad because he needed food. He quickly made a U-turn in the parking lot and backtracked to a drive-through, grabbed several burgers and several coffees, and made it back to his apartment. There he sat down, brought up his laptop, hooked up to the internet, and logged on.

He accessed the campus video feed and found the relevant dorm room, where he hit gold. There he watched a man walk down the hallway. Several other students were coming in and out of their rooms, laughing and joking, but all of them completely ignored this one man.

He knocked on the door, where Carly lived, and it opened almost immediately. She smiled at her visitor and opened the door wider to let him in. The man's features were hard to see on the video feed. He texted Hatch. **See if we can clean this up and get an ID.** He gave him the date and time stamp for the Smith Hall feed.

He waded his way through the rest of the video to see if the guy came out again. He did, but he had a different look to him. Now he looked older, stood taller and straighter, and he quickly walked away. Corbin sent the relevant time stamp for that part of the video to Hatch as well.

"Kudos for the disguise," Corbin muttered to himself. But it wouldn't be enough. Not now that he knew that somebody had deliberately targeted people he was talking to. And he was damn sorry about Carly. She obviously knew her visitor, as she'd let him in, but how did she know him?

And with that question in another text message sent off to Hatch as well, Corbin started to eat his burgers. *Good thing we have a tail on Louise.* But Corbin's mind raced, wondering just what the hell was going on here. And, if Nellie's kidnapping wasn't connected to these other women, where the hell were those women?

CHAPTER 3

N ELLIE WOKE THE next morning, still in the same ugly
darkness. Except this time, she had a better idea where
the bathroom was. She got up slowly and made her way
there. She found the light switch, and, as soon as it turned
on, she turned and checked out the bedroom and frowned.
She was still alone. There was no sign of the other woman.

Nellie used the facilities, came back out again, and sat
down on her bed. The food must be drugged. And the
problem with that was, she needed the food, but she didn't
want anything to happen to her baby. When the door
opened, the other woman walked in and sat down beside her
in her own bed in a nonchalant way.

Nellie stared at her in shock. "Are you okay?"

She looked over at her and nodded. "Yeah. Why not?"

But her voice held such a bitter tone that Nellie knew
something was going on. "What happened? I woke up, and
you were gone."

"Yeah, that happens sometimes," she replied. "Nothing
good comes from this place."

"What about your daughter?" she asked gently. "How is
she?"

"Alive," she said succinctly. "And that's about all I can
say." And, with that, she laid down on her bed and rolled
over.

Nellie wasn't sure whether her roommate had been warned to stay quiet or if something else was going on. When the guard arrived with plenty of food for her, she studied it carefully. She looked up at him and said, "Could you at least reduce the drugs a little bit? I understand that you're trying to keep me complacent and quiet, but I really don't want to hurt the baby."

"Nobody will hurt the baby," he snapped, and then he was gone.

She winced. *Great, go ahead. Eat your drugs, Nellie. It won't matter because, hey, they'll be looking after your baby.*

The other woman rolled over. "You really don't get it, do you?"

"Well, I get some of that, but I'm obviously not getting all of it."

"They'll take your kid away from you," she said flatly. "As soon as you give birth, it won't be yours anymore."

Nellie stared at her in horror. "Is that what happened to you?"

"No, I already gave birth before I got here, but I was picked up with my daughter, and now they are weaning her off me."

Nellie hated to ask the question burning at the base of her throat. "But do you know what they want to do with our kids?"

"Adopt them out."

Nellie's hand went to her chest to control her breathing after the initial shock. "What if we didn't want them adopted?"

"It won't matter because you don't get a choice."

"And if we refuse?"

"I presume that's why the other woman is dead," her

roommate said. "You have to sign forms, giving your rights away."

"Oh, God," Nellie gasped, staring at her. "I really don't want to give birth in this place."

"No, I wouldn't either." She looked around their room. "But, hey, you figured out how to get a light on."

"Was that supposed to be a test?"

"I don't know, but they sure as hell didn't show me."

"It's in the bathroom," she shared.

The woman looked at her in surprise, then nodded. "I guess I'm just used to the darkness. When you're up all night long with kids anyway, I never bothered turning the lights on anymore."

"Will you sign the forms?"

"I don't have any choice," she snapped, then reached a hand to her head. "God, I feel like shit."

"I'm sorry. Did they drug you?"

"They're drugging all of us," she snapped. "So just in case you think you're special, ... you're not."

Nellie winced at that because, of course, it had been an instinctive thing that maybe, maybe for some reason—maybe as a parliament member's daughter—these kidnappers would treat her better than the other people. And, of course, it wasn't to be, no matter how much Nellie wished it were otherwise. "I wonder why they took me, while I'm pregnant," she pondered out loud.

"I think they're hoping it might be easier on the kids."

"I guess that's possible, but it's a lot harder on the mum."

"But they can get rid of the mum faster too, before she connects with the child," she snapped. "Who knows? They might just shoot you, as soon as you give birth."

Something about this other woman's tone made Nellie wary of so much bitterness directed at her. "I'm not sure what's going on," she whispered, "but I'm not your enemy."

"You're sure as hell are not my friend either." The other woman gave a bitter laugh. "For all I know, you're some sort of a mole. They're certainly treating you better than they treated me."

She stared at her in shock. "I'm sorry, but I don't know anything about that."

"No, of course not. You're also pregnant." She waved her hand toward Nellie. "And they won't do anything to hurt the child."

Which was the one and only saving grace, as far as Nellie could see, because, as long as they were looking after the baby, she had a couple months to get through. Hopefully before that, somebody would rescue her. At that, she sent a mental message to Corbin. *Get here fast.* "Have they threatened you?" she quietly asked the other woman.

"Many times. They've told me what'll happen if I fight. They also told me what'll happen when they're done."

"When they're done with what?"

"Weaning my child," she replied bitterly. "Again don't think you're anything special. They're taking a different tactic with you. The only reason I can think of is the fact that you're pregnant. So that pregnancy is protecting you right now, but it won't forever."

"Got it." And Nellie did. Horror slid through her. She had to get out of here. "Do you know what they're doing with our children, outside of adopting them?"

"No, I don't. The only good thing I know is, they're looking to get families who can properly care for them."

"Have we been determined to be not good parents or

something?" she asked cautiously.

The woman rolled over and grimaced. "I don't think they even know us." She stared at her in shock. "And that's not something I want to contemplate."

"Then why did we get picked?"

"Because we had the requirements. A kid for me and, in your case, pregnant with a kid. That's all I know."

"Why not take a woman who's got like eight kids then?"

"They're too old. Our children have to be a certain age." She gave another bitter laugh. "After that, it's too hard for them to adapt to the new family."

"I see," Nellie muttered, her heart sinking. "And we're killed off?"

"Sure, so the kids don't remember us. Or so no one else finds out about us down the road."

"Meaning, they can't allow us to live because we'll talk."

"That would be the theory, yes," she said, her voice brutally honest. "Unless you have someone who will help you get out of here fast, you need to come to terms with it."

"How will you come to terms with the fact that you'll be killed, when your kid is okay to not be around you anymore?" Nellie asked, bewildered. "That's not possible."

"When you figure it out, let me know," she snapped, "because, otherwise, I don't have any answers, and my time is coming up pretty damn fast." And, with that, she rolled over and faced the wall and refused to talk anymore.

⚓

HATCH CALLED. "WE have an ID on Carly's killer. And an address for him. He has a brother. We'll run him down too."

"Where am I going?" Corbin immediately got up,

snatched his gun, placing it in his shoulder holster. Grabbing his jacket, he raced to his vehicle.

"You're only about five miles away. I'm sending you the address."

"Good, I'm on my way." At that, Corbin's phone dinged with the location.

"Better find him before somebody kills him."

"Oh, I get it," Corbin murmured, "and believe me. I want to ask this guy some questions, so I need him alive."

"I know, but our worried parliament member is all about being certain you get whatever you need right now to ensure he gets his daughter back."

"Right." Corbin reached the apartment building and sent a picture of it right away to Hatch. "Does this look like the deal?"

"Yeah, that's it. There is alley access."

"Okay, I'm heading there now." He slipped inside the apartment building, via the back entrance. There was no security, nothing to stop him from going in. He shook his head at that, not at all sure why anybody would live in a place like this. Particularly if he did the kind of work that Corbin did.

Although, if there was no security, either physical or digital, Corbin could slip in and out on his own. Nobody to watch his movements. Upstairs on the third floor, he found the room he was looking for. What he needed was the element of surprise. With that thought, he took out his tools and had the lock undone in seconds, then he slipped inside and stood still. A TV blared just around the corner, yet no one was visible. To the left he heard somebody in a conversation.

"Yeah, yeah. I know. I know. I took care of it."

Corbin peered around the corner and saw one male on a ratty couch.

"Of course I did. ... Nobody saw me. You know that. ... No, it's fine. You just keep those women quiet, and we'll be all good. ... No, yeah, I understand they've got multiple adoptions lining up. It's not my deal, and you know that too. I'm only doing this because you needed help. I'm not getting further involved. Especially with anything pregnant." The guy laughed. "That's like the worst. I can't believe you got involved to this extent."

Silence came, then the voice continued. "Yeah, I know. He promised you a big load of money, but you know something? This bullshit about not paying us just never stops. They always talk big money. I haven't seen any payout happen yet. You keep doing these shit deals."

More silence followed, as this guy listened to whoever was on the other end of the call.

"No. I know, but, bro, ... you're just heading down a pathway that I don't want to go. I took care of the problem this time, yes, but that's it. I'm not doing you any more favors. I have to go. My show is back on TV." With that, he hung up, tossed down his phone, and slumped onto the couch. When Corbin moved into his line of sight, he said, "Jesus Christ, what the hell?"

Corbin stepped forward, grabbed him around the neck, pinned him in place, and whispered against his ear, "Yeah, that's what I want to know too. What the hell are you doing killing young university students, who are just talking to law enforcement?"

The other man froze and then started swearing.

"Yeah, you're not as good as you think you are." Corbin snapped, "It was pretty damn easy to track you down. Now the cops want to talk to you, but I wanted a moment with you first."

The other man gulped and said, "I didn't do anything."

"Liar."

"I am not."

"We have video of her opening the door to you, and, when you came out, you're looking different but not all that different."

The other man growled, "Fuck off."

"No, I'm not going anywhere." Corbin grinned. "However, I do want to know where the hell these women are— the ones you were just talking about to your buddy."

"I'm not telling you nothing, and you can't make me."

"I can, and you won't see daylight for a very long time."

"Says you," he sneered. "I can take you out and disappear. The cops will never find me."

"They already know to look for you. The camera feed came up really clear."

"Bullshit, I'm better than that."

"Nope. I can tell you that my techs are much better than you ever thought you were." Corbin laughed. "If you haven't upgraded your skills over the last few years, you're just a loser, ... a bottom-line loser."

"Shut up," he muttered, gasping for breaths.

"I don't have to. I'm not going anywhere until you talk."

"And I ain't talking. Sounds like we're at a stalemate."

Corbin thought about it for a moment. "I guess I'll go pick up your brother too. We'll see how that piece of shit handles interrogation."

"You leave my brother alone." He swore heavily. "Shit. Shit. Shit."

"Nah, he's the one who got you this job. He's the one

involved with the women. He should be a piece of cake."

And, with that, Corbin hit the pressure point on the guy's neck and knocked the man unconscious. Within minutes, Corbin had him tied up and secured, had pulled his wallet to confirm ID—Earl Embry—and he called Hatch. "I need an address for the brother. I overheard the telephone conversation, and Earl's brother has got the women somewhere. I need someone here to keep an eye on this prisoner. He's secured, but I don't want to leave him alone. And I've got his phone too," he added, while grabbing it from the unconscious guy. "I'll take some snaps of his contacts and recent calls, texts, then leave the phone for the cops."

"Your partner will be there in a second."

"I wondered if I would even get one." A sudden knock came on the front door. "Shit, I got company."

"In this case it's a good thing. It's who we've been waiting for."

He opened the door to see Aiden, an old navy buddy. "Aiden?"

"Yeah, that's me," he muttered. "I was supposed to be here earlier today."

"Oh, shit. Are you my partner?" He stared at his old buddy.

"If that's okay with you." He smiled. "I've missed out on a lot. Bring me up to speed."

"That's okay. You've got perfect timing. I really need you to stand guard on this guy." He pointed at the unconscious prisoner. "I will let Hatch fill you in, and I am going after the brother."

"Who is this guy? And why is he tied up and unconscious?"

"Earl Embry. He just killed a student on the university

campus, and his brother is involved in kidnapping mothers and kids."

"No problem. He's not going anywhere. You go do your thing," He looked at him and shook his head. "Typical Corbin."

"What do you mean?"

"You leave my guy unconscious and tied up. What's for me to do?"

"Hey, I'm not taking any chances. If he wakes, get him to talk. We've got to find these women and fast."

"Oh, I don't doubt it," Aiden murmured, "and the sooner, the better."

As Corbin walked out the door, Aiden sent him a text.

Anything I should know about this asshole?

Yeah, he's a piece of shit and seriously involved. And, with that, he raced over to his vehicle, his phone ringing.

"We are working on this," Hatch said, "also take care to not step on any toes."

"Aiden is here. He'll keep an eye on my lovely prisoner. Have you sent him the files? So he can get up to speed?"

"Yeah, I've sent him the files. He'll catch up while you're out."

"Good," he murmured. "Better if you're sending law enforcement there so Aiden can come help me on this end."

"As soon as we get some law enforcement whom we can trust, absolutely. Of course that's not always the easiest. But we'll have someone there soon."

"Okay, good." Corbin looked at the brother's address on his phone and immediately plugged it into the car's GPS and headed out. He noted a second vehicle parked off to the side and wondered if it was Aiden's. He quickly phoned Aiden.

"Did you drive in?"

"Yes, that blue truck in the parking lot is mine."

"Good. I'll need you to haul your ass to me, as soon as law enforcement hits your corner."

"Will do. They are taking their sweet time, but I got somebody at the door now."

"Good enough. I'm about four minutes away from the new address, which I've already sent to you."

"Okay, got it. Give me a few minutes, and I'll be on your tail in no time."

And, with that, Corbin hung up and double-checked his GPS. The address was just around the corner. He made a couple quick maneuvers and was right outside what looked like a really low-end boarding house. He frowned at that. "You know what? For all these weird jobs your brother said that you had lined up, looks like you aren't doing so hot."

He exited his vehicle, headed up to the apartment number that he had on file. As he got there, the door was open, and the guy inside was singing at the top of his lungs. Corbin winced at that because, chances were, this brother was high as a kite. Corbin walked in and called out, "Hey, man, your brother sent me."

The guy stopped singing, looked over at him, and smiled. "Good. Glad he changed his mind."

"Absolutely. Although he's still not sure about these women."

"Of course not." The brother laughed, a high-pitched sound that hurt Corbin's ears. "He thinks I can't do anything. Calls me a fuckup every time I talk to him. But he doesn't know."

"What doesn't he know?" Corbin asked, trying to humor him.

"He doesn't know that this is the big one. This is the score of a lifetime. I'll be living high on the hog, and he'll be the one begging me for work."

"I hope so, for your sake."

"Yeah, don't you worry." He gave Corbin a fat grin. "Plus I gave them two more names they can go pick up." He squealed with laughter. "Man, how sweet is that?"

"Oh, nice. Your brother is probably trying to figure out how he can score too."

"He should. He was always a good scout, but he got soft. He doesn't like to target women anymore."

"Yeah. Well, he went to bat for you though, didn't he?" Corbin added in disgust, "When you needed him."

"See? He doesn't like to even talk to me about shit like that." He looked at Corbin and asked, "Man, you got a weapon on you?"

"Of course I do."

"Oh. … I don't deal with weapons very much. I'm more of a scout type, you know? I go hunt the women, find the ones they can use, and then I hand over the names and don't have to worry about anything else. They do all the dirty work. Me? I get to take my money and run with it."

"How many do you have to give them though?"

"Hah, you just want in on the same deal," he replied. "See? I might help my brother, but I don't know you from shit."

"No, that's true," Corbin agreed. "I was just wondering if they were a tiny-ass operation that you have to worry about getting your money or if this was a big deal."

"I don't really know. So far, there hasn't been any problem with the money. As soon as I give them a name, and it checks out, and they pick her up, and it's all confirmed, then they pay me good money."

Corbin rolled his eyes. "Wow. So why are you living in this dump then?"

"Well, … the last two I gave them I haven't been paid for, just a little deposit." He frowned, then immediately cheered up. "But I will. I will soon."

Corbin nodded and stared at him. "I suppose you just text them because they never answer phone calls."

"Yeah, exactly. They get back to me with a yes or no, and then we go from there."

"Well, how do you know they didn't pick up your no responses? Maybe they just don't want to pay you for those."

He just stared at Corbin, then shook his head. "They wouldn't do that. We've been working together for a while, for … months."

Corbin nodded again. "Ah, okay. You trust them then."

"Yeah, of course I do. Of course I do. You know what? My brother says I can't trust them, but then he doesn't trust anybody."

"That's because he's probably been burned."

"Yeah, he has had a couple bad deals." He sniggered. "Not me though."

"I imagine he's struggling right now. Worried, you know?"

"How so?"

"His face got caught on the cameras."

"What do you mean, his face got caught on the cameras?" he asked, staring at Corbin in shock.

"So you don't know? That chick he just wasted, … new cameras were set up on that dorm floor," Corbin said in a conversational tone. "His face is on the video feed."

"No way. My brother is too smart for that shit. He's

great at disguises."

"It's one of the reasons why he sent me over here. He's in a spot of trouble, and he wants to know if you can give him a hand or not."

"What kind of trouble? Better not be trouble because of my deal." He glared at Corbin. "Because, you know, that's one of the conditions. This job has to be simple. Quick and easy. No drama and no trouble. This has to go perfectly."

"No, of course not. That's the only way these guys know how to operate, right? I mean, trouble is bad news for everybody."

"Yeah, you're not kidding."

"You can ask your brother, if you want to," Corbin said. "He went to lie down. He's feeling kind of sick."

"Hey, that's not my brother either. He doesn't do sick."

"Until he realized that his face is all over the cameras. And now he's trying to see if he can skip town."

"So he sent you to ask for money? Like bloody fucking hell. ... I'm not giving you money. You'd just keep it yourself. My brother is a big boy. He can handle whatever he's gotten himself into. He's gotten away from this kind of trouble before."

"I don't think he can this time."

"Yeah, why not?"

"His face, ... it's out there now. Cops are looking for him."

"So what? It's a dorm. A ton of people will be there, coming and going."

"Absolutely there is. But it's not like he goes to university, and he's the only one who went inside her room, and the only one who came out. Dead chick in the meantime."

"Yeah, that's his style." He sniggered again. "I can't do

the killing. It's really not my thing. But it's his." He shook his head. "I'm still not giving him any money. My brother is fucking loaded."

"Loaded?" Corbin stared at him, shaking his head. "Have you looked at the dump he lives in?"

"He's still got way more money than I've got. He should know better than to be asking me for money."

"Unless he can pin any of this on you."

The guy stopped, stared at him, and swallowed hard. "No, no, no, no. He can't mess this up. He can't. It's too good of a deal right now."

"Except he's in trouble, so, good deal or not, I highly suspect it won't make a damn bit of difference pretty soon."

"No, no, no. That's not allowed." He thought about it for a brief moment. "Look. ... Tell him I'll meet him at the old place."

"As long as he knows where that is."

"He'll know. Meanwhile ... I'll get him some money. But I can't give him much because I haven't been paid yet."

"What? Haven't been paid for any of them?"

"No, not yet. They have got to make some sales first."

"Oh, shit. Are you sure you're in with a decent group?"

"Of course I am." And then he winced. "But not if they find out my brother got caught. I was supposed to take care of the girl, but, because I don't do the killing, I hired him."

"Of course you did, and I don't blame you. Besides, killing is one thing. Killing innocent students at school? That's a whole different story."

"Right. I mean, there's just no way I could do that." The kid reached up and pulled at his hair. "My brother doesn't give a shit. He kinda takes it in stride. But, ... well, I really can't do that."

"Okay then, so what do you want me to tell him?"

"Tell him that I'll meet him at the old place. I'll bring some money, and he needs to make sure that nobody comes with him."

"Of course. I don't think your brother is that stupid."

"No, he isn't." He looked at Corbin suspiciously. "I wish he'd told me that you were coming."

"I'm not sure what I can tell you about it, except that he's in trouble and that he needs help. Tell me where this outfit is, and I'll see if I can get you your money."

"I can't do that. But shit. … For him to need my help, it's got to be bad."

"You don't think getting pinned for murder isn't bad enough?"

"No, not for him. He's always got a bolt hole to go to."

"Okay, so how about the fact that you're connected and that he's trying to warn you?"

"Well, that, in a way, yes, could hurt me," he said, all signs of laughter gone from his face. "But shit. That's not making me feel any better. I can't have anything messing this up."

"Then help him get out, out of trouble. Tell me how to help you get your money."

He thought about it for a long moment and said, "You know what? I am gonna need some ID from you."

"Fine." Instead of searching for his ID, Corbin pulled out his gun. The guy looked at it, back at Corbin, and whispered, "Damn."

"Your brother is already on the way to the cops. He's turning you in right now. I was hoping that maybe you'd give him some money to help keep you free and clear, but you know what? It's always the same shit. *You don't want to help your brother."*

"I do," he cried out, "but you're the one with the gun."

"Yeah, because I also don't have a problem killing people"—Corbin glared at him—"particularly if they need it. So where are these women now?"

"I ain't telling you that, no way. I'll get my ass kicked."

"Yeah, you'll get your ass kicked anyway. I want names and dates, and I want them now." And, with that, he cocked the gun.

CHAPTER 4

N ELLIE TWISTED IN bed, trying to get comfortable. When that didn't work, she got up and walked around, for the baby's sake.

As she did, the other woman shook her head at her and rolled her eyes. "Like that'll help."

"It can't hurt," Nellie muttered.

"Maybe not but it's just ridiculous to think you'll get out of here alive."

"Maybe." She glanced back at the picture her kidnapper had given her. "I still don't know who the hell that guy is either. Yet my imagination tells me that I should."

"It's not like he'll be any help."

"Oh, he might," she murmured. *Now if only she had a way to contact him. Although she wouldn't be much help, as she didn't even know where they were.*

"How the hell will that happen?" asked the other woman, who snorted as she rolled over.

"I'm Nellie." She'd tried to introduce herself several times, but the other woman was less-than-friendly. However, as her words registered with her roommate, her shoulders shook ever-so-slightly. Nellie realized that this woman was dealing with an overrun of emotions, just as crippling as those felt by Nellie. This woman's child was on the other side of that door and already knew what her future held.

Nobody needed to deal with this kind of hell.

The fact that Nellie was pregnant wasn't making it easier on her—or her roommate. If anything, it made Nellie more emotional. At least the other woman wasn't as bitter as she had originally appeared to be. Nellie felt it was just her roommate's way of coping with the trauma.

As was her silence and her refusal to state her name.

Nellie once again studied the features of the man's face in the photo—who she'd already come to memorize—and shook her head. "Any help will have to come from my father." Nellie sagged at the end of her bed, reaching again for the photo.

"Even if your father gives a shit and even if he's doing something about it doesn't mean there'll be any way to find us. This has been going on for too long now, without anyone finding out, so what's changed? Nothing. If anybody was looking or had any success, they would have found us long before you were ever taken."

Nellie winced at that. "I hope you're wrong"—she reached behind to rub her back—"because that would really suck."

"Think about it. Some of the women have been here longer than I have."

"If he's planning on keeping me until I'm due," Nellie said quietly, "that would be more than another couple months too."

"And if the baby arrives earlier? What then?"

At that, Nellie stared at her roommate in horror, as Nellie's mind filled with reasons why that would happen.

The other woman shrugged. "You have to consider everything. Time is money for them."

"I get that." Nellie grappled to get her mind wrapped

around time-saving methods. "I really don't like the way you're thinking though. I've never been one to foster a Pollyanna attitude. In fact, my life has been full of more shit than anything."

"Yeah, reality is a bitch, and I'm still better off if I face that."

It was pretty hard to argue with that kind of logic. "Is there any way to get word out? Have you ever been outside? Felt fresh air? Heard anything to help identify our location?"

The other woman shook her head. "No, no, no, and no. Do you think we haven't all thought about it?"

"I'm sure you have, and we already know what happens when you fight. I'm just wondering if there was anything else to consider."

"Nope, any rescue will have to come from somebody inside, either getting cold feet or a falling out among thieves or something ..." She groaned in frustration. "It won't come from us doing anything."

"That sucks," Nellie replied. Almost on cue, she heard an odd noise outside. Yet the other woman didn't seem to note the sound. Her roommate rolled over and faced the wall, pretending to be asleep. It wasn't a bad idea, but Nellie waited, sitting up, wishing her back would not ache quite so bad.

At the same time, she would take it because considering anything else could be so much worse. What she really wanted was to be free and to be back at her own place, safe and healthy.

And she admitted to herself, back with her father again.

The door opened, and the same captor walked in, holding a covered tray. The door remained open. Obviously somebody else was outside the door then. He saw her sitting there and nodded. "Good, you are awake. You need to get up and walk around more."

She nodded. "It would help," she admitted, wanting to keep on his good side. She got up and walked around, holding her back. "Is that food?"

"Yes. I didn't know if it's good for the baby to have coffee, but I thought maybe a cup of tea would help you settle better."

"Thank you," she said in surprise. He looked over at her, gave her a bashful smile. She wasn't sure exactly what was going on here, but she certainly wasn't above milking the nice attitude. When he set down the tray and uncovered it, she smiled at him. "Thank you very much. It looks good."

And, fact was, it didn't look bad. He placed one plate on her bed. Nellie could have been given moldy bread and leftover food sourced from Dumpsters, but this was a sandwich with whole grain bread, and it looked like ham or something in between. She held out her bottle and hesitated. "Could I have more water, please?"

"Of course." He took it and walked to the door.

She assumed somebody stood on the other side of the door, but she hadn't seen anybody there yet. However, when hushed voices came on the other side, that confirmed her suspicion. She just waited, not moving back to her original spot, yet trying to appear compliant.

When he returned with a full bottle of water, he still didn't close the door.

A test? She wasn't prepared to do a whole lot. Not in her condition. Plus she had no intention of risking her child.

At the same time, she wouldn't let them take this baby away from her. She'd gone through too much for it. Now when he returned, she smiled and thanked him again. She opened the bottle and took a drink right away. And then she started to rub her belly, as if there had been a stab of pain.

"You okay?" he asked in concern.

She nodded. "Baby is just kicking."

"Ah," he said, with a bright smile, "that's good then." She didn't say anything, just nodded again. He picked up the tray, with the second plate of food, and pointed to the other woman. "When she wakes up, this is her food."

"Thank you."

He walked to the door. He looked back at her, hesitated, and she waited, hoping for him to say something, *anything*. But then he stepped out, closing the door behind him.

As soon as the door shut, the other woman rolled over and snapped, "See what I mean?"

"I do." She nodded. "And I'm definitely not above using it, if I can get us out of here."

"But there's no guarantee that he has any ability to help us."

"The door was open the entire time, so I don't know if that was a test or whether somebody was out there, holding it ... and watching us."

"Could be either. Could be both." The other woman sat up. She looked at the food and sighed. "More sandwiches."

"Yes, but it's food," Nellie pointed out. "It's more than I expected, more than I got yesterday."

Her roommate grimaced and frowned at her. "*Pollyanna.*"

Nellie shrugged. "You must know that we would stay alive for quite a few days on half this food, so given this much is a help."

"Maybe," she muttered, staring at Nellie. "How do you know any of this?"

"I'm doing my master's thesis on it," she said. "To become a nutritionist."

"So you're a student?"

She nodded at that. "Yes. Which means, they are hunting for women at the university."

"My name is Jewel, by the way," she said abruptly, finally softening. She lifted her sandwich and took a bite. "I'm not in school. Haven't been in school for a very long time." She stared in disgust at the sandwich. "If I were smarter, I would have stayed there, but I let no-good men sidetrack me. I got hooked into my first bad-boy romance when I was sixteen. I took off with him cross-country on a motorcycle." She shook her head. "God, that was a long time ago."

"Yet you had fun, didn't you?"

She snorted. "For all of five minutes, until he dumped me at a truck stop in California and never came back. I'd been asking for food and canned drinks and bottled water and then bathroom breaks the whole way. I guess he decided that was too much trouble."

"Ouch." Nellie winced. "I gather you weren't pregnant back then, yet I can relate because it seems like all I do now is go to the bathroom."

"Isn't that the truth." Jewel gave Nellie a ghost of a smile.

"So how did you come from the States to be here?"

She hung her head. "I was stupid yet again and was a drug mule." At Nellie's frown, Jewel explained it a bit. "Wow, you are naïve." Nellie flushed. With a shake of her head, Jewel continued. "I wanted to go abroad. The only way I could afford it was to carry drugs." Nellie's confused expression made Jewel growl. "Man, are you some sheltered rich kid?" Nellie didn't bother answering. "You swallow the drugs in these special bags, so drug-sniffing dogs can't detect them."

"Oh my God." Nellie was getting an education here.

"Problem was, my body rejected the bags earlier than expected."

"Where?"

"In Heathrow."

"What did you do?"

"I told the truth, gave up my contact in the States. Promised them and me that I'd go straight after that. I was on some supervised probation and had to answer any questions they had later. And I've been good ever since. Really I have." She paused, gave a big sigh. "Then I got pregnant, and that guy bailed too. The really stupid thing is, I was planning on giving up my daughter for adoption because I didn't think I could handle it—being a mother, a role model, taking care of something so small and vulnerable—yet now all I can think of is what kind of future is facing her without me to protect her."

"One with you," Nellie said in a firm voice.

Jewel looked over at her. "How can you be so upbeat and positive?"

"Well, we're alive. We have food. We have water. Plus now I know people are looking for us, and, although you may not have the same vote of confidence as I do, I still feel like we'll get out of here."

"You haven't been here long enough to have that beaten out of you yet." Jewel yawned, before she took another bite. She chewed and chewed. When she finally swallowed, she said, "I sometimes have to force down the food."

"That's because you're looking at it as a replacement for something you really want," she stated simply. "Try looking at it as being a gift, which it is." She stared straight into Jewel's eyes. "It's a gift of survival right now. And, as long as they're trying to keep us alive, then they're not killing us."

Jewel looked at Nellie sharply, but she took a bigger bite and nodded. "It's all about attitude, isn't it?"

"It's mind-over-matter thinking, and it's a good attitude to have," Nellie said quietly. "And, if there's one thing we need to do, it is to stay positive, to stay cooperative, and to give whoever is out there looking for us a chance to get to us."

"You think that guy will find us?"

"There's certainly a can-do attitude to him, isn't there?"

"He looks like one of those men on the covers for a romance novel," Jewel said, a derisive tone in her voice. "I inhaled those books when I was a kid. My mom was a big fan. So, when I fell hard, I fell *really* hard, thinking he would be my hero."

"At that age I'm not sure any heroes are out there." Nellie laughed gently. "But we do look at the world with stars in our eyes, don't we?"

"Maybe no heroes are out there, but you can bet that I felt betrayed nonetheless."

"That's the downside of romance novels like that, isn't it? You want what they're all talking about, and so you go looking for it. Yet half the time what you really wanted was what's right under your nose."

The woman snorted at that. "You do have a persistent Pollyanna attitude."

"Maybe," Nellie said cheerfully. "But you have to stay positive right now. Because things might get pretty ugly, and we have to stay strong."

Almost on cue came shouts and a scream next door. Nellie stared over at Jewel. "I would say that that's a classic example of how things could get much worse," she whispered in a heavy tone. Jewel remained silent. Nellie added, "And that's the warning to not fight, I presume."

"Absolutely. There's no winning in this case."

"Well, if there's no winning," Nellie stated firmly, "we need to do everything we can to not fight and to give whoever's coming after us as much time as he needs to get here."

Jewel turned toward Nellie, but a glimmer of hope seemed to be in Jewel's gaze. And then Jewel slowly lowered her glance and took the last bite of her sandwich. She put her empty plate on the tray. "I'm sorry for being such a shit when you first got here."

"Hey, I understand. I mean, maybe if I was here for a couple months, I'd be the same. Which is depressing because I do feel positive that we'll get out of here."

At that, Jewel looked down at the picture of the man on the sheet of paper. "I hope for your sake it's him."

"Why is that?" she asked, with a note of humor.

"Because, of all of us in here, you seem to be the only one who's positive enough to keep us sane. It feels like it's too late for me."

"I don't know that *sane* deserves getting a guy like that. I'll be looking for a rescue, yes, but whoever it is, I won't care. I'll just be damn grateful."

WITH THE YOUNGER brother subdued, Corbin pulled out the kid's wallet, took photos of his ID and some credit cards—expired—and sent them off to the Mavericks, then put in a quick phone call to Hatch. "Now I've got Darwin Embry, the brother who searches for the women and submitted the names for consideration." He cast a quick glance at his prisoner on the floor. "How's Aiden doing?"

"He's on his way to you."

"Good. This guy needs to talk, and he needs to talk fast."

"Are you serious? He's the one who puts in the orders?"

"Yeah, Darwin is a scout. He searches for the women, hands over their names and photos to these kidnappers, and those guys decide if they'll collect them or not. If they're collected, … he gets paid. Well, after the moms are killed and the children are sold presumably."

"Jesus, what a piece of shit."

"Yeah, not only that, Darwin here won't help out his brother either," he added, with a note of humor, as he looked over the unconscious man to his right. "I'd like to beat him up a little bit more, but it only took one pressure point to knock out the asshole. I feel like I should leave it to Aiden's soft touch."

"You absolutely should. You might have to add a little pressure to get him to cooperate in the end, but Aiden can handle the beginning."

"I suspect it'll take more than a little bit of cooperation for this kid. Darwin seems to think he's onto the sweet money-making deal of a lifetime and doesn't want anything, including his brother, to screw it up."

"You mean, supplying these women?"

"Yeah, these other guys involved may be the ones physi-cally taking the women, but Darwin's just as involved. He only cares about getting paid." Corbin reached up to rub the back of his neck. "So this guy among these assholes takes the cake."

"Right. We'll leave something for Aiden to beat up. You know how he feels about assholes like that."

"I know. I know. Keep me posted."

"Yeah, you too."

With that, Corbin hung up and turned to look at his prisoner, who was blinking up at him from the floor.

"What the hell happened?" Darwin asked, as he tried to stand, only to find his arms and legs were tied up. He stared at Corbin, and then his gaze widened in horrified comprehension. "You," he spat out. "What the hell do you want?"

"Well, your brother has been picked up by the cops. So not so sure I want anything from you at all."

He stared. "Seriously?"

"Yep. After all, you wouldn't help Earl. Don't worry. We're busy reminding him of that too."

Darwin shook his head. "I don't know what your game is or what the hell you're doing in this whole mess, but you don't know what these guys are like. You need to untie me and let me out of here."

"Or what?" Corbin crouched in front of his captive.

"Or they'll kill me."

At that, Corbin stared at him. "When you lie down with the dogs, you better be ready for the fleas. Why would they kill you?"

"Because they won't tolerate any interference." He struggled against his restraints. "I mean it. These guys are serious."

"Of course they are, Darwin. They're kidnapping women, stealing kids, committing murder right, left, and center. It's very serious. You think the cops aren't just as serious about putting a stop to it too?"

"I don't give a shit about the cops," he cried out, with a force that surprised Corbin. "You don't know what these guys are like. There are no second chances with them. And how do you know my name?"

Corbin wiggled this kid's wallet in front of his eyes. "Haven't you figured out that you've already reached the end of your usefulness?" Corbin asked him. "Probably as soon as you hired your brother to do your dirty work."

The guy sagged back down on the floor. "But how would they know that?" he asked, as his gaze went wild. "I know that they didn't want me to hire out the job, but it was my brother. I knew he was good for the job."

"Of course you did, and, like they already told you, *Don't do it*, but you completely disregarded that and decided to go for it anyway. I mean, if you won't follow their rules, ... why should they follow any rules either?"

He stared at Corbin in horror. "No, no. You don't understand. These guys mean business."

"Yes, so do I, in case you hadn't figured that out by now."

Darwin looked around in a panic. "What do you want? I don't care what it is. Just tell me what you want, and let me out of here."

"I want to know everything you can tell me about these guys."

He snorted. "Why? So you can get your ass kicked?"

"Or I can do some ass-kicking." He gave a grim laugh. "What are they doing with the kids?"

"I don't know. You know what? I don't give a fuck either," he cried out. "Let me out of here. *Let me out!*" And he struggled in a panic, until he kicked over a floor lamp with his efforts.

"That didn't help, did it, Darwin?" Corbin muttered, staring at him.

"You don't understand what these guys are like," he gasped, breathing hard.

"Yeah, so you keep saying. No, I don't, and I can't say I'm too thrilled that they're even out there. I find more-than-enough assholes are out there in this world."

"Yeah, they're assholes ..." he whispered. "I'm telling you. You don't want to jerk around with these guys."

"No? At the same time, I'm really not too bothered about them because I have you in front of me right now."

He sagged in place. "Please just let me go," he begged. "If they saw you come in here, it'll make them really worried."

"In that case"—Corbin gave a feral grin—"they'll really love the fact that my buddy is on his way."

"No, nobody else can be here," he cried out. "Don't you get it? They will kill me if they think I talked."

"I'm sure they *will* kill you. You've already talked. To your brother. Told him way too much. I mean, the cops want to talk to you real bad now. You've got an inside line on everything these kidnappers do, and you could make their games dangerous as hell for them."

The kid stared at Corbin, then blinked. "That's right. I do know things, don't I?" A crafty look entered his gaze. "So maybe," he said, "maybe I should do a deal with you to let me go and then do a deal with them. If I lead you to the women, maybe they will kill you."

"They won't give a shit about me"—Corbin waved his hand—"not once they realize you talked to me."

"But they don't know I talked to you."

"Unless I tell them so."

At that, Darwin started to panic again. "Look. I don't know what game you're playing at," he roared, as he tried to get free of his ties, "but you don't know what these guys are like."

"Yeah, yeah, yeah. I've seen guys like this time and time again, and I bet they're all the same. They're assholes. They've got an agenda, and they take out everybody who's been helping them. But you can't seem to get that through your head." Corbin stared at Darwin, wondering if anybody was really this stupid. Everybody thought that they were indispensable.

"They won't do that to me. I ... I've been in this business too long. ... I'm a supplier. I go way back with them."

"And that's the trick"—Corbin nodded—"*too long.* You know where the bodies are buried. You know what they're doing. You're the one who's been tracking down these women, and they're paying you for those names—or at least *promising* to pay you," he added, with an eye roll. "You don't even know how many they're paying for, and, in theory, you don't even know if they're ripping you off."

"They wouldn't do that. We have a long-term relationship and all that."

"Right, like that matters."

"It does matter." Darwin glared at Corbin. "You don't understand loyalty."

"Not loyalty like this," Corbin said calmly. "But I really didn't think you were that gullible. You do realize they have been ripping you off from the very beginning, right? That's what they do."

At that, Darwin just glared at him.

"And your brother? Earl? Is he likely to talk when he's in jail?"

"Nope, he ain't gonna talk." His prisoner tried to lash out with his fists and then his feet but got nowhere, as both were securely tied.

"You know that how?" Corbin asked.

"Because he also knows the score."

"Ah. So you think your brother'll keep his silence when the cops talk to him, instead of turning witness against you for a lighter sentence?"

"He knows these guys will kill him."

"Does he though? Did you give him any details?"

Darwin thought about it for a moment, and then a bright smile lined his face. "You know what? That's a good point. I didn't give him details, so he can't tell the cops nothing."

"Except that he killed somebody on your behalf."

"Yeah, but I could just say it was all bullshit." Darwin was evidently warming to the idea, looking remarkably pleased with himself. "That's a really good line to take on this one. Thanks for that."

"Oh, I don't know about you being welcome and all, but, hey, as long as you seem to think that is something your brother will appreciate, whatever."

"No, he won't appreciate it, but then he shouldn't have gotten caught. Everybody knows that. As soon as you're caught, you're on your own."

Corbin nodded. "And is that the same rule for you, when you get caught?"

The guy shifted restlessly. "No, I'm different."

"Ah, of course *you're* different." Corbin gave a knowing nod.

"You don't have to make it sound like that." He glared at Corbin. "When you've got a long-term working relationship, you know who to trust."

Corbin shook his head at him in disbelief. Was this guy for real? "*Right.* So how many women have you procured for them? How long is a long-term relationship to you?"

"Half a dozen, more, although I don't know how many they picked up out of all that," he added slowly, "because they still owe me."

"Owe for how many?"

He stared at him for a moment. "For a bunch," he said calmly enough, but a worried look crossed his face.

"Meaning they haven't paid you for *any* yet, have they?"

"No, but they were just waiting to get paid on their side."

"Of course they were." Corbin shook his head, wondering at the absolute stupidity of this guy. "And you're expecting them to follow through with it, right?"

"Follow through with what?"

"*Paying* you." Corbin stared at his prisoner. "You expect them to still pay you?"

"Of course. I mean, I've given them more than a half-dozen names. They need those women."

"Sure, maybe they did, but they have the women now, so why do they need you? And, if they don't need you, why pay you?"

Subdued now, Darwin frowned, studying Corbin. "I know what you're trying to do—but you're wrong. We've been working together too long for them to screw me over."

"*Right.*" Corbin waved a dismissive hand. "You've got a *special* relationship with them."

He nodded. "I do. Hey, I worked hard to cultivate it." But his voice was starting to lose conviction.

"I'm sure you did, and how did you find these guys?"

"A buddy of a buddy. I got word that somebody was looking for some women. I put in a call."

"So you didn't care what happened to these women, right?"

"They're all bitches," he sneered. "Every woman is a bitch, so what do I care? They're only good for one thing, and most of them had kids. They had already been breeding." At that, he laughed. "Besides, the specifics were pretty clear."

"Yeah, right. Single women, a couple kids."

"Young, healthy, and fit but in a spot—vulnerable types, who didn't have anyone to care if they went missing. Who nobody gives a shit if they lived or died."

"Nice guy, aren't you?" Corbin's stomach twisted at the shopping list. Not that Nellie fit the list.

Darwin shrugged. "It's not like they didn't take advantage of a lot of guys. Do they even know who the fathers are for those kids?" he snorted. "Those women deserve everything they got coming."

Inside, it was all Corbin could do to hold back from hitting the guy square in his face. To think that guys like this were out there and were operating on colleges was unbelievable. But to think this asshole believed his own BS was something else yet again. Corbin kept his calm and asked him, "So, once you hand off the targets and the women's schedules, then what?"

"Then it's up to these guys. It's no longer my problem. I mean, I'm a finder. A supplier. All I'm doing is scouting out chicks they might be interested in."

"Right, *chicks that they might be interested in.* I wonder how MI6 will look at that."

"It won't matter because I ain't talking."

"No, of course not." Corbin sighed. He didn't bother telling Darwin that he wouldn't live long enough because no way in hell these guys he worked with could afford to let him live. But somehow that was a truth that seemed to be completely missing in this guy's brain. Corbin looked at him. "I suppose you used your phone to text them."

"Yeah, sure," he snapped.

"That just implicates you even more."

"Nobody'll be tracking the numbers."

"They didn't give you a burner phone, did they?"

"No, why would they? I prefer to use my phone anyway."

A knock sounded at the door. Corbin walked to it and peered through the keyhole; it was Aiden. He opened the door, let him in, and asked quietly, "Anybody see you?"

"Possibly. A vehicle's parked outside."

"Good." He looked over at the kid. "Somebody's outside watching your place, Darwin."

He paled and immediately struggled against his bonds again. "Let me go. Let me go, please. You don't understand. I have to explain it to them."

Aiden looked over at Corbin. "Are we letting him explain anything?"

Corbin shook his head. "Nah," and he quickly explained what Darwin had been up to.

Aiden turned, looked at their prisoner, and sneered. "Jesus, so you set up these women for whatever nastiness these guys have planned for them?"

"I didn't do anything. I just found a couple pretty chicks. That's all."

"Sure, a couple pretty chicks who fit parameters these guys were hunting for. You just became a procurement tech," Corbin snapped, creating the term right on the spot.

The guy looked at him in surprise. "Oh." Then he brightened. "Hey, I have a fancy job title."

Aiden sucked in his breath, but Corbin patted Aiden on the shoulder. "Don't worry about him. He ain't going to live past tomorrow."

"He won't live much longer today either. They saw me come in here."

Corbin agreed. He looked at the prisoner. "So what else can you tell me about these women?"

"Nothing. I told you that these guys give me a list. I find it. Later I give them a couple prospects, and that's it. I get paid."

"How do they pay you? Transfer to your bank account, cash, what?"

"It's supposed to go into my bank account." He grinned. "That's a whole lot easier and less hassle for me that way."

A half snort erupted from Aiden, but the kid ignored it. Corbin continued. "But again, you haven't been paid yet."

"No, because they're waiting for the payment for the sales of the kids to go through."

"You know they killed one of the mothers, right?"

He shook his head, shrugged. "Well, it wouldn't have been one of my choices for women. They were perfect."

"Right. Well, let's check." Corbin pulled out his phone and brought up the picture of Mary. "You find this woman for them?"

Darwin looked at her and nodded. "Yeah, she and her kids were buying groceries one day at a store close to the campus. Only carried what she could. Didn't even get a cart. On a hunch, I followed her, and there she was. ... She was struggling to hold on to a couple kids. Like how is that a life for the kids?" he sneered in disgust.

"How's that a life for the kids when their only parent is gone? That person, that single mom, was trying desperately hard to improve her situation in order to get a better life for the kids."

"They'll have a better life now." Darwin shrugged. "These guys will see to it."

"Right, there's some kind of twisted Messiah message. What do you know about the buyers? Are they like heroes?"

He looked at her photo and frowned. "She's really dead, huh?" Darwin stared but just with a bored curiosity, as if he'd never seen a picture of a dead person before.

Aiden looked over at Darwin, then spoke to Corbin. "Now that I'm here, what do you want to do with him?"

Corbin glanced at the kid and asked Aiden, "Did you take in his brother?"

"Yeah, Earl has been picked up. He's downtown in jail."

"Good enough. Let's take this guy down too." Corbin immediately relieved the kid of his phone and began taking several screenshots of his contacts and most recent texts and calls.

At that, Darwin looked at him in horror. "No, no, no, no, no, no. Remember that part about me not surviving?"

"Yeah, we got it." Corbin nodded. "Remember that part about I don't give a shit?" Corbin finished his fishing expedition into the kid's phone. Now he sent all the screen captures to Hatch for the team to cull through. He looked over at Aiden. "Let's go. We'll get him off our hands, so we can hunt down the rest of this group."

Aiden looked at him, with an eyebrow raised.

Corbin tossed the kid's phone on the floor for the cops to find easily but not within reach of the kid. He'd didn't want him to alert his buddies. "I'm waiting on the team to get back to me with details, but hopefully there'll be something concrete."

Almost immediately his phone buzzed. Corbin looked down at the text message and smiled. "Absolutely lovely. Time to get going." His statement was followed by a knock on the door, and they let in two cops.

Corbin explained what was going on. "You can take Darwin's statement, and we can cover the rest of the interview later. We have to go now."

They handed the kid off to the cops, but not before Aiden took a picture of the cops who were here. "Just so that we know who we're handing them over to."

The cops flushed angrily. "Don't worry," said one of them. "We're not a part of this, and this piece of shit is not going anywhere."

"Good," Corbin murmured in a hard voice. "Make sure he gets to jail." He stepped out the building and saw where Aiden had parked. Corbin looked over at his partner and said, "We need to trim down to one vehicle."

"Yeah." Aiden nodded. "This one will be picked up soon. I've already arranged it."

Corbin nodded, hopped into the front seat of his vehicle, and watched as the two cops brought out the kid.

They didn't make four steps when they heard a sharp *ping*, and the kid took a bullet, right in the forehead, tumbling backward to the ground.

CHAPTER 5

W HEN THE DOOR opened the next time, a different man walked in. Nellie stared at him, gave him a tentative smile. He didn't even look at her and walked right back out, and her hopes sank. What were the chances that they had decided to change the jailers because the previous one was getting too friendly? Definitely not what she wanted to consider, but, at the same time, it made sense. If she were the jailer, she would have made sure of it.

To even think of herself in that position made her sway onto the bed, exhausted and terrified. Just that little kindness from the one jailer had kept her hopes up. Absolutely nothing about this scenario would she ever take part in. But, if she were a commodity, that was absolutely how they would treat her.

With her hope sinking, the man returned and held out a bottle. She accepted the water quietly, but he walked over to Jewel and jerked her to her feet. Even though she had been sound asleep, she came up crying, as if her instincts had been to expect the worse, and he just smacked her hard, making her gasp and quiet down instantly.

He looked over at Nellie and gave her a cruel smile. "Just in case you think you're somebody special, you're not."

She didn't say anything but watched as he dragged Jewel from their room.

"Oh, dear God," Nellie whispered to herself. She heard loud shrieks on the other side of the door, then ... silence. She bowed her head. Obvious no one was around for miles to hear their screams. Jewel's ordeal was an awakening call, and all it did was reinforce the fact that Nellie needed to get the hell out of here and fast. She sidled up to the door and listened with her ear against it. She heard muffled voices.

"That's all you have to fucking do," one man snapped. "Treat them like the cattle they are."

"They're not cattle," the other man argued, his voice trying for a more reasonable tone. "They're scared and alone. These are good women."

"If you can't do the job, we'll find somebody else."

"Hey, come on. You know I can do the job," the reasonable one protested.

"Then don't be so damn friendly with them. You can't be friends with them."

"It doesn't cost anything to be nice," he replied quietly.

She knew this scenario wasn't good for him or for her. She had to find a way out before this ended up a one-way street for her and her child. *That she wouldn't let happen.*

When the door opened again, she looked up to see the friendlier guard.

He looked at her and winced. "She's okay, you know?"

Her eyes widened. "Are you sure?" she whispered quietly. "She didn't sound okay."

"She is under guard and absolutely fine." He shrugged. "I can't tell you more than that, so it has to be enough for now. More than that doesn't go down well here."

"And yet isn't this to be expected? You're keeping this woman prisoner. You've taken away her child. How is she supposed to react?"

He nodded. "I get it. I guess this isn't what you thought would happen when you got up yesterday."

She stared at him in shock. "No, it absolutely isn't." She looked behind him. "Is she out there?"

"No, she's been moved to another location."

"Oh," she whispered. Now she was alone. Holding fear at bay was way easier when there were two. Alone? ... That left her feeling way worse, vulnerable.

"As long as she behaves, ... she'll be fine."

Nellie didn't say anything because absolutely no way she would believe that, not after what she'd just seen and heard. "And me?" she asked, her voice faint. "Will I be fine too?"

He immediately rushed to reassure her. "Yes, of course."

"No." She shook her head sadly. "There is no *of course* in this. I heard what the other guy said. You're being nice and all, more so than you're allowed to be."

He stared at her and then quickly handed her a bottle of water. "Take it."

She accepted it and sagged onto her bed. She felt the tears in the back of her eyes, but she had no way of knowing what to do at this point. With a jailer and another asshole somewhere farther down the line, escape was impossible. She looked up at him. "Could you even help me if you wanted to?" she asked sadly. "Or any of us?"

He shook his head. "I can't do that," he murmured, so low that she barely heard him. "They'd kill me too."

She nodded slowly. "I believe you." And she did. She sagged onto her bed, feeling the tears choke her throat. He was right. They would kill him, so why would he risk his life when he didn't even know who she was? There was no rhyme or reason for it, no logical explanation for him being nice to her, yet he walked over to her side and whispered,

"I've tried to persuade them to let you go, but they're pretty stuck on keeping you."

"Why would you do that?"

He shrugged. "Because I don't agree with this."

She stared at him. "You don't agree with it *now*."

He flushed. "It wasn't supposed to be like this, and it wasn't supposed to go quite so badly," he muttered, then glanced back to the door. "I can't talk. Later ..." And, with that, he disappeared.

She stared at the door, wondering if it was even fair to have hope that this jailer might help her. But hope was something that lived eternal—as long as she fed it—and it would keep her alive and keep her sane, if only she could believe that he meant what he had said.

He could let her go.

He could absolutely be the link that she needed to get out of here. He could also be the instrument of an early death—for her, her baby, and even him too. She couldn't forget that. His sense of self-preservation had to be alerted to any danger he was in too. She also didn't know what he would want in exchange for helping her, ... if he helped her.

He'd said it wasn't supposed to be like this. What did he mean?

Nothing about this was normal, so anybody who got into it must have had some make-believe scenario going on in their heads where they thought any of this would work out to anybody's benefit. Particularly to the women's benefit. When he went out the door, it clicked shut, followed by a double click. She groaned as she sat here and stared at the locked door.

"It'd be nice to know what's outside of that door," she muttered aloud, but her chances of finding out anytime soon weren't great.

Just then the door burst open, and Jewel was thrust inside. She collapsed to the floor, crying out in a horrific manner.

Nellie raced over and helped her to her feet and back over to the bed. "Good God, what happened?"

She sobbed. "They found somebody for my daughter. They're selling her."

Nellie stared at her in horror. "Good God. There must be something we can do." She glanced around the room, trying to figure out what, if anything, they could do.

"If you think this won't happen to you, you're wrong," Jewel whispered, and she started to bawl.

"Has it already happened? Has she already been handed over?"

Still sobbing, Jewel shook her head. "No, no, but soon. They're making arrangements right now."

Nellie nodded. She stared at the door, walked over, and gently tested it.

"Like that'll work," Jewel snapped. "Do you think I haven't tried that time and time again?"

Nellie turned and lifted her finger to her mouth and whispered harshly, "*Shhh.*"

Jewel fell silent, as she stared at Nellie. Then Jewel hopped up and came beside her and whispered, "What are you trying to do?"

Nellie didn't say anything but listened with her ear against the door. Only silence greeted her. She heard no voices, no sounds—nothing. Then she heard footsteps—soft, muffled footsteps, almost like someone sneaking up. She pulled Jewel away, and both raced over to their beds and hopped in. But this time, when the door opened, it only partially opened, then closed again—only … not quite. Then the footsteps receded.

Jewel looked over at her, her mouth wide open.

Nellie put her finger against her lips again and whispered, "Maybe … just maybe somebody is on our side." And, with that, the two women raced to the door.

CORBIN PULLED UP to the address that Hatch had sent him.

"What's this address for?" Aiden asked.

"Hatch tracked it from one of the numbers the kid called in the last few months. Darwin is too stupid to use burner phones, but it seems these guys he's working with are always using a different burner number." Corbin pointed down the road. "At a store up ahead, they have been selling more than the normal amount of these phones."

"Would they be so stupid as to buy burner phones locally?"

"Considering they could buy them off the internet or anywhere else, it's possible. However, this is a lead. So we have to check it out."

"That we do," Aiden agreed. "What about video cameras?"

"I've got Hatch looking into it," Corbin muttered, as he studied the location. "The guys have to be close. They don't want to move the women and children until they're ready to sell them because any transportation will be dicey."

"Yeah, but what's dicey is also keeping kidnapped women and young children quiet, so they must have a vacant location to hold them." Aiden studied his friend for a moment and then nodded. "What would you pick?"

"Somewhere quiet with a deep basement, where they could scream, and nobody would know."

"Right, that's a given," Aiden agreed. "It needs to be close to services, to food, but big enough in a town that nobody will understand why they're buying more food than they should be."

"If anybody even gives a shit," Corbin said. "I mean, if they're doing this right, they'll just be anonymous faces in a sea of faces."

"And yet this kid brother was working for them, and he seemed to be a local."

"Because they have to have somebody on the streets, so to speak. Besides it's his face in the public eye. They're hiding behind him."

"Who was just terminated."

"Right," Corbin confirmed, and then neither of them spoke about it. They knew exactly what would happen to Darwin, but they had hoped it wouldn't. Even with Earl in the police station, he still might not live to talk. However, when you saw these kinds of criminal business alliances, too often someone realized they didn't need to share the profits with so many others. "I figured it would end up this way, as soon as I realized he hadn't been paid yet. And yet he kept making excuses."

"At one point in time you would think the brothers would have figured it out."

"Do you ever wonder how our species even survives when there's so much lying, cheating, and just lack of honesty everywhere?" Corbin asked, as he continued to look about his surroundings, trying to find where the women could be held.

"Absolutely."

They headed to the electronics store first. When that became a dead end, with nobody willing to talk about anything, Corbin found a panhandler outside, and he walked over to him, held out some money. "I have a few questions. Some more money for some answers."

The guy immediately looked wary. "Answers about what?"

"Looking for a guy who has been coming back and forth, buying burner phones."

He shrugged. "How would I know?"

"I think you would know. Have you seen the same people coming and going lately?"

"Sure. Lots of the same people come and go," he replied, eyeing the twenty pound note in Corbin's hand.

"Anybody odd?"

"No, not odd." He shook his head. "Some people do come in and go in a big hurry."

"Yeah? Anybody in particular?"

He looked over at Corbin and Aiden and asked, "What's this about?"

"Some men kidnapping women and children."

At that, the panhandler's face thinned. "I had nothing to do with any of that." He started swearing. "God damn, don't you try to pin that on me."

"We don't think you did that, but we think that you're here all day, every day, and chances are you might have seen something important. Like the guys only buying burner phones."

He sneered.

"More than that," Corbin added, "I think you've probably noticed suspicious behavior and wondered."

At that, the panhandler fell silent and nodded slowly.

"Somewhat, yeah. A van was here the other day. Two guys were in it. Then one guy ran into the store, while the other guy didn't like being left alone. However, the first guy pretty well yelled and screamed at him, although it was done quietly. I still heard enough to realize the second guy didn't want to stay there in the van."

"Of course not," Corbin waited. "Did you hear anything?"

The panhandler stared off in the distance. "Just something about we went to too much trouble for this to get screwed up."

"Right, that would fit too."

"But I don't have any proof of anything these guys were doing. I just saw a van."

"What about the plate?"

The panhandler stared at the twenty and looked up at Corbin and the back at the twenty. Corbin shook his head, pulled out his wallet, and found another twenty. The guy nodded. "I got three off the plates," and he reamed them off.

"That'll help," Corbin noted. "If you see that man or the van again"—he handed him a card—"let me know. There's a lot more money where that came from."

"They really stole some girls?"

"Multiple women but, more than that, they've also stolen their kids." His voice nearly growled, as he added, "One of the mothers' bodies showed up dead."

The guy shook his head. "It's a messed-up world out there, man."

"It is, indeed. You stay safe."

And, with that, they headed out again. Back in the vehicle, Aiden driving this time, Corbin quickly reported to Hatch about what they had found.

Hatch started a trace on the numbers. "Okay, we've got several options," Hatch said, "but the most likely van with no windows was stolen."

"Of course it was." Aiden pounded the steering wheel. "It feels like we're out of time here."

"Yeah, me too," Corbin agreed. "But we can't focus on that. We have to stay focused on what we've got going on right now."

"And I get that, but my instincts say we need to move," Aiden said to Corbin.

"Look for likely locations, warehouses, condemned buildings." With that, Hatch hung up.

"We should search the area where the van was stolen from," Corbin suggested.

"Why would anybody take a van close by?" Aiden asked.

"Convenience." At that, Corbin's phone buzzed. He read the text message out loud. **The van was found in a warehouse, after it had been stolen two days ago.** "So they used it just for the job and then ditched it."

"You and I would do that," Aiden noted, looking over at his friend.

"Yeah, we sure would. Still, if it's convenient, then they are close by. Because moving all the women and children has got to be convenient too."

"True. If we don't get a handle on this fast, they'll find an area of town not very convenient and move them."

"No, I get it." And, with that, Corbin punched into his GPS the address where the vehicle had been stolen, while Aiden drove along per the directions. Ten minutes later Corbin noted, "It's a commercial district. I wonder what brought them here to steal a vehicle?"

"Honestly it could be just as simple as the fact that theirs broke down," Aiden suggested.

"Hey, it's possible, but we're grasping at straws."

"Of course we are. That's all we have to grasp at right now."

As Aiden drove by the surrounding area, Corbin surveyed the commercial district closely, looking down alleyways and sides of each warehouse. He caught a glimpse of one woman helping another woman step through a narrow rusted door of one warehouse close by another. He yelled to Aiden, "Stop."

Aiden immediately hit the brakes and pulled off the side of the road. "What's the matter?"

And Corbin pointed in the direction where he saw the women.

Aiden whistled as he turned around toward the women. "Okay now, hang on a minute. Are those the ones we're looking for?"

"I think so," Corbin murmured. "Leave the vehicle here." They quickly bolted from the vehicle and headed toward the women. As soon as the women caught sight of them, they started to run away. But one was obviously pregnant, and the other one looked like she was suffering in a big way.

Corbin reached out for the pregnant one, and Aiden grabbed the other. Corbin slapped a hand over the woman's mouth, as she started to fight and scream. "Stop. Stop, damn it. I'm here to help."

He didn't even slow down but just tightened his grip around her, picked her up, and raced back to the vehicle. As soon as he got her into the front seat of the vehicle, Aiden came up behind him with the other woman, who didn't look to be in very good shape. Corbin immediately opened up the door to the back seat of the double-cab truck, while Aiden popped her inside and called out to Corbin, "You drive."

Corbin hopped into the driver's seat, with the woman seated in the passenger seat, frozen, staring at him. He looked over at her and asked, "Nellie, by any chance?" She seemed in shock.

"You're the man who my father hired."

"Yeah." He frowned. "How do you know?"

She pulled something from her pocket and handed it to him. He stared at his image. "Well, good Lord. How come you have that?"

"One of my jailers asked me if I knew who you were and that you were looking for me."

"Well, at least you could say no, that you didn't know me."

"True," she replied, "but I have to admit that I hung on to this picture because it gave me hope."

He looked over at her, and, in a gentle voice, he said, "It worked. We're here."

"Let's get moving," Aiden said. "This woman needs medical attention." And directly behind them, a bullet was fired and then another. Their back windshield exploded.

Corbin sped ahead and slammed his hand over Nellie's head and pushed her down. "Get down. Get down." A vehicle charged up behind them. "It'll be a rough ride," he snapped, his tone grim. He looked over at her and gave her a feral smile. "At least you are with us now."

"Yeah," she whispered, from her crouched position, "but we're hardly safe."

"No, not yet." He veered off the road, heading across a parking lot. "But you need to hang on tight, particularly with that belly." He looked over at her. "Did they hurt you?"

She shook her head. "No," she whispered, "but Jewel is hurt." She lurched higher trying to see Jewel. "We have to go back." He stared at her in surprise. She cried out, "I mean it. We have to go back. Kids are still there and more women."

He nodded. "I know, but first we'll get you guys away."

Another round of bullets was fired into their vehicle. She shrieked and ducked.

"Remember that part about staying down?"

"What about you?" she snapped, from her crouched position.

He just smiled. "They might get me, but chances are in my favor." He immediately turned several corners and several more, and then he tossed his phone to her. "Let the cops know who you are and where you are."

"I don't even know where the hell I am," she snapped, but, her fingers trembling, she was already dialing. As soon as she got through, she relayed the message and gave a couple street names off an intersection as to their moving location, as coherently as she could.

Just then another bullet rang out.

"We're being shot at," she cried into the phone. "They're trying to kill us. They're chasing us, and they're shooting at us."

Corbin didn't listen to the rest of the conversation, as his focus was on making sure that these assholes didn't run them off the road.

As soon as she was off the phone, he told her to punch Speed Dial 1 on his phone, then put it on Speaker. "Hatch, we need backup. We're being fired upon. We have both Jewel and Nellie. There are more women and children still to be rescued, before these assholes move them." He quickly gave Hatch their general location, adding, "Jewel needs medical care, and I have no idea on Nellie. She says she's fine, but I'm not sure I believe her." At that, she snorted beside him, and he grinned. "She's not as bad as she could be. Put it that way. ... No. We picked them up as they were sneaking out of a building, grabbed them, and ran. ... We were seen, and the kidnappers are in pursuit."

"I've got nothing within ten minutes," Hatch said.

"Cops, ex-cops, military, retired military, anybody?" Corbin swore, as another bullet came his way, and he looked over at her and yelled, "Hang on." He took a hard corner to avoid the gunman in that vehicle. "I think another vehicle's coming after us now too. I need a place to hide."

"Now that," Hatch murmured, keys clicking hard on his end, "I might give you. Hold on."

It took less than two minutes, and he came back. "Follow my instructions."

And, with that, he led them on a continuous path at top speed. "Take a sharp right and pull into the garage," he said. "The doors will slam tight behind you."

CHAPTER 6

NELLIE SLOWLY SAT upright in the vehicle, as Corbin parked the vehicle in a garage, the door slowly lowering. Corbin was now out of the driver's side door, running around to her side, telling her, "Go, go, go, go." Corbin pulled her from the passenger seat, hustling her out of the vehicle and into the adjoining building.

"I thought we'd be safe now," she cried out.

"No. It won't take them too long to find us here. Now pick up the pace, and let's go."

"I was so grateful that you were on your way to rescue me, but now I could definitely change my mind."

He looked at her and then laughed. "Too bad, but I'm what you've got. Plus, in my line of work, getting to safety means running through some fire, whether gunfire or a forest fire. So quit complaining and just move. Besides, your friend needs help. *Remember?*"

Nellie nodded, noting Jewel was already being carried into the building with them. "What's up with coming here?"

"It's a temporary safe house for us. My boss sent us here, so we have some time to regroup." He looked over at her. "There are times to argue, and there are times to do as you're told without hesitation. We learned that lesson early on in the navy. It's saved my life many times over."

She got the message. She stayed quiet, as he quickly led

them into a hallway. As they got onto an elevator, he punched in a series of buttons which made no sense to her.

"How do you even know where you're going?" she muttered.

"My contact on my phone is telling me." He looked over at Aiden. "How is she?" Aiden carried the unconscious woman. "Did she get hit?"

"I think she's basically okay," Aiden said quietly, "but I need to do a full check." He looked back at Nellie. "Do you know what happened to her?"

She shook her head. "She had just returned to our room. She was distraught because they just found a place for her child."

"Don't worry. We'll be going back in very quickly," Corbin confirmed. "The plan is to rescue everybody."

"The kidnappers must know that we're missing—given the guns shot at us just now—so they'll move everybody."

Corbin nodded. "Yes, that's a big possibility. We've got satellite coverage for the area right now. So we're tracking all movement. If they move, we'll know."

She stared at him. "Seriously?"

He smiled to hear such hope in her voice. "Yes, my boss is on it right now."

"Are you sure?"

"Yeah, the cops have been called. You yourself did that, and we have an awful lot of resources at our disposal right now. I also have somebody else who wants to talk to you."

"Who?" She stared at him, a dazed tone to her voice. All she could think about was maybe this nightmare would be over soon. The fact that they had found a way out of the kidnapper's building on their own was huge, and then Corbin finding them? … It was almost too good to be true.

"Later. How did you get out?"

She shrugged. "I think one guard deliberately left the door unlocked for us," she whispered. "I'm afraid they'll kill him."

He looked at her steadily for a moment. "That's possible, but he'd have known that too."

She swallowed. "I was hoping no one would have to die."

"They've already killed one woman we know about so they could get full possession of her two children. And there's a good chance that Jewel could have been the next one."

She stared at Jewel in the other man's arms. He wasn't showing any strain from carrying the not-so-tiny woman. "I hope she's okay," she said anxiously. "She's been through a lot."

"Do you have any idea how many other women there are?"

She shook her head. "At least two more in the room beside us, per Jewel. She also spoke of one dead woman who had been there earlier."

He nodded.

"I'm not sure the mothers were all killed though." He raised his eyebrows at that statement. She shrugged. "I didn't get any clarification on that issue. I so want to see Jewel get her daughter back."

"We're working on it."

The elevator opened suddenly, and they moved rapidly down to another door. Corbin punched in a code, and a series of lights flashed, and the door popped open.

She stared at him. "I don't know what you just did, but damn."

He smiled. "Go on in." And, with that, he let Aiden in, carrying Jewel.

Aiden laid Jewel on a bed inside the closest bedroom. "I'll have to check her over. Give me a minute."

With that, Corbin pulled Nellie back out, to give Jewel some privacy. "Come on. Let's go into the living room."

"But he might need us. I don't want her waking up and freaking out."

"You let him handle it. He's a navy medic. And he's damn good too."

"Yeah, but a medic is not a surgeon."

"He has done more surgeries than most surgeons," Corbin explained. "Aiden is a surgeon in all but name. He chose to continue doing this kind of work instead of staying in the navy."

She didn't even know what to say to that. She held up her shaking hands.

He nodded, walked over, and didn't even give her a chance to say anything but pulled her into his arms and just held her close.

"I don't need that," she said, trying to get free. But that huge expanse of comforting chest and the fact that he'd been the one to rescue her and that she was finally safe, altogether was obviously magical because she burst into tears and buried her face against him. He held her closer. When the tears finally dried up, she lifted her head and whispered, "I'm so sorry."

He smiled, brushed her hair off her face. "What for? Being human? For going through a horrible ordeal and now being safe? Somebody who's in shock and still trying to deal with the changes in her life? You've been a kidnap victim for how many days now? You don't have anything to be sorry for or to be ashamed of, and I'll bring it up once, and then I won't bring it up again. You are pregnant, so it's a well-known fact that hormones will play a huge part in your reactions."

She stared at him and smiled. "I'll try very hard to not get too emotional on you."

He chuckled. "I don't know about that. I know that you'll do the best you can, but *Baby* here"—and he gently patted her belly—"will play an important role too."

She stared down at her stomach, wrapped her arms around it, curled up against his chest, and whispered, "We both thank you."

"You're both welcome."

She didn't move; she didn't do anything but cuddle closer, knowing she was finally safe. "I don't know what the hell happened to my life. I'm just so damn grateful that stage is over."

"Did you recognize anything or anyone while you were there?" he asked.

"No, nothing. I just woke up in this locked room. Like, one minute I was on campus, and the very next? I was in that locked room. One of the men was really a decent person, and, I know it sounds terrible to say, but the other one was a piece of shit." She shuddered. "But this one nice guy, I'm pretty sure he deliberately or accidentally didn't secure the door, so that we had a chance to get free. My gut says that he did this deliberately, and I don't even know how to explain it."

"No explanations necessary," he muttered. "It's possible that he realized that he had to do something—perhaps seeing a pregnant woman pushed things for him too far, or it's possible he didn't realize the other woman had been murdered."

She stared at him. "You found her?"

He nodded.

"That confirms what Jewel said too. That terrified me. I stayed compliant, so I didn't end up the same way."

"Exactly. You're alive. You're well, and Baby is doing okay. Granted, we're not clear and free of danger yet, but we are in a whole lot better scenario than we were twenty minutes ago."

She smiled, looked around, then back to Corbin. "I don't even know where you're from."

"I'm Corbin Wallace, US Navy. A special division, black ops," he said quietly.

"You are a long way away from America."

Corbin nodded. "I got to travel the world with my parents when I was younger. Now, with my navy connections, I still get to travel." He smiled. "And, yes, as I'm sure you already understand, your father had something to do with this."

She winced. "Of course he did. I'm grateful, even though things aren't great between us."

"That's between you and him."

She stared at him and smiled. "Meaning, you don't want to get between us?"

"Meaning that, whatever disagreements you had," he said calmly, "probably are no longer valid, given what you've just been through."

"That's a sobering thought too." She shook her head. "Believe me. While I was a captive, all I could think about was the fact that my father wouldn't know how absolutely sorry I was. I know he was worried, and I kept pushing him out of my life, instead of finding another way to handle him."

"And I'm sure he's going through something similar too," Corbin murmured.

She laid her head back down against his chest. "Do you do this for all your rescued damsels in distress?"

He chuckled. "I don't know about that." He gently rubbed her back, his chin resting atop her head. "That would keep me pretty busy." She lifted her head and looked at him. He shrugged. "I've been blessed to have a hand in some pretty amazing rescues."

"And that sounds like stories worth telling, when we have time."

"Maybe. Right now we'll keep you safe, and we'll do our darnedest to get you back home."

She leaned back slightly, so she could look up at him. "That would be an absolute miracle right now, but we have to rescue those kids and the other women. I'm seriously worried about them."

He nodded. "I get that. Believe me. Even as we speak, a full-on raid is being planned to rescue them all. Even if they don't catch the kidnappers, the satellite will track them. They won't get away with this."

"No." She took a deep breath; then she voiced the fears that were choking her. "What if they decide that all the women and children aren't worth this and kill everybody? What if they decided to cut their losses and run?"

CONTEMPLATING SUCH AN option, Corbin looked up to see Aiden standing in the open doorway to the sickroom. "She's awake and asking for you," Aiden said, studying the two of them with interest.

Immediately Nellie broke free of Corbin's arms and asked, "Oh, my goodness, is she okay?"

"Well, she certainly isn't feeling better, but the fact that she's free helps. She's worried about her daughter."

"Yeah, me too." Nellie made her way to the bedroom.

Corbin got up and headed over, so he could see the reunion between the two women. Jewel opened her arms, and Nellie fell into them, both of them crying.

When Jewel had a moment, she looked over at the men, and her eyes widened. "Oh, my goodness." Her gaze traveled from Nellie and back to Corbin. Then she chuckled.

"Look at that. He really did come to our rescue."

CHAPTER 7

N ELLIE REACHED OUT and gently brushed back Jewel's hair. The other woman looked exhausted. Her face was puffy, and her eyes were red. One cheek was swollen, and old bruises colored half her face. "How are you feeling?"

"Pretty rough." She looked over the two men. "What about the kids and the other women?"

"We got you away first," Aiden explained and walked closer. "You went unconscious as soon as we got you into the car, so I'm sure you have no idea that we were fired upon several times, while trying to get away."

"No, I don't remember that," she murmured, "but kids are still there, like my daughter, and other women."

"We're on it. It's not just us. We have teams out there."

She sagged in relief. "Dear God, I sure hope this is over now." She looked around. "Can we call anybody? Can we call families and friends?"

"Not yet," Corbin said instantly.

Immediately Jewel's gaze switched to the men, and she frowned suspiciously. "What? Why not?"

"Because we don't know if there was any connection from those in your lives to the people who did this."

Her gaze widened. "Oh, God, are you serious?"

He nodded. "Until we have a little bit more in the way of answers—or, at least, until we have the kids and the women picked up, we stay alert. Nobody gets wind of anything yet."

She took a deep breath. "Okay, fine, but their rescue needs to happen fast." She swallowed several times. "I just want my daughter back."

"How old is she?" Aiden asked quietly.

"She's one," Jewel replied, pain in her voice. "She's just one. And they've been trying so hard to wean her away from me and to make it so she doesn't even remember who I am or cares about me." Her voice broke. "They told me today that they had a family where she would go, and she'd be so much better off without me." She started to sob, ... big noisy sobs. "I know I haven't been the best mom. I've been trying hard though. I really have. I'm trying to get back to school and to get a better job, and it's just so damn hard."

"Hey, hey, hey," Nellie said quietly, gently rubbing her shoulder. "That's not today's issue. You were doing the best you could. It wasn't their right to take your daughter away from you."

She started to cry even more.

Nellie looked over at the two men. "Is there any coffee? Food? We were kept on short rations but it was enough to keep us alive."

"I'll get something." Corbin pulled out his phone and started sending texts.

"And we need," Nellie added, as he turned away, "clothes, showers, anything will be appreciated."

He nodded. "Give us a minute and remember. We might have to still run fast again."

She winced. "Right. This is just a place for the moment, isn't it?"

"Possibly, but let me see what we can do." And, with

that, the men left Nellie and Jewel alone.

Nellie looked down at Jewel and gently rubbed her shoulders. "We got this far. Let's go the distance and trust."

At that, Jewel gave her a brief smile. "There's that optimism of yours again. I didn't even think we'd get out of there alive."

"Well, I figured we would." Nellie grinned. "And we're here now. Obviously it's not a done deal yet, but we're in a hell of a lot better spot than we were, not even an hour ago."

"We are," Jewel murmured, "but nobody else is."

"I know, and I'm trying hard not to think about all that because we can only do so much. We took the chance to escape, so we can get help for the others. Just remember that."

Jewel looked over at her. "Do you think that guard left the door open on purpose?"

She nodded. "Yes, I do. What I don't know is whether they killed him for it."

At that, Jewel's gaze widened and then nodded. "I can see them doing that—assholes." She shifted uneasily on the bed. "In the kidnappers' minds, they won't think even their guards had a choice. When you think about it, loyalty will be everything. And if they were already slimming down their own numbers ..."

Nellie shook her head. "Plus, for their criminal enterprise, selling children would be more expedient than waiting for me to give birth. That takes more time, more money, a lot of patience, and no guarantees that the baby I have later will meet their requirements." She frowned. "I looked at adopting myself—from a legal entity of course. However, they have stringent governmental regulations and requirements, and not everyone can get approved."

Jewel looked at her in surprise. "But why? Obviously you can get pregnant."

"Sure, I know that now. Yet back then, the thought of going to a sperm bank was kind of revolting."

The woman stared at her. "Is that how you got pregnant?"

She nodded. "Yes, only no one knows."

"Oh, my goodness." She shook her head. "That's not at all what I imagined."

"No, I'm sure nobody did," she murmured. "But I had just about had it with relationships going nowhere. Men who seemed to be complete losers. You know what I mean."

"Yeah, I know what you mean," Jewel muttered, with a headshake. "I never had any luck in that department either."

"I always figured that pregnancy wasn't something that I wanted to fool around with. I also wasn't sure about a sperm donor either, but then—when I got to pick so many different things about the genetics—well, it almost became like candy."

"I'm not going to lie, but that sounds weird," Jewel said, staring at her.

"It is weird. It's a very strange process," Nellie agreed. "Yet it works and, in my case, works well. It had the very much desired results."

"And does the father get to know about your baby?"

She shook her head. "No. He gave the sperm, was paid, and signed forms, giving away all rights. So he did his part of the bargain, and I bought the result."

Jewel just stared at her. "That's such a weird concept."

"It was for me too for the longest time, but, whenever I had a relationship, and it blew up in my face, I just couldn't see myself missing out on one of the best experiences of life. I really wanted children. And failing at the relationship thing and with my father against me getting pregnant in particular," she added, "I didn't let it stop me."

"No, I can't see anything stopping you." Jewel laughed. "You're very determined."

"When I found out I was pregnant," she confessed, "I was alternately horrified and thrilled and then horrified all over again. And, of course, I went through that whole *I don't deserve to have kids* judgment. *I don't deserve to be a mom at all*. I beat myself up really bad then," she noted, more to herself than to Jewel. "Life beats us up, and, if it doesn't," Nellie said cheerfully, as she slowly stood, "we beat ourselves up. Come on. Let's go sit with the guys."

"Sure, why not?" Jewel added in a dry tone. "It's not like we have anything else to do."

"Have some faith. A little bit goes a long way."

"I sure wish I could have seen the look on your face when you saw who it was that came to the rescue."

Nellie laughed. "I have to admit that I didn't really believe my eyes for a moment."

"Will you tell him that you were mooning over his picture?"

She felt the color sweep over her cheeks. "Heavens no," she gasped, looking at Jewel in horror. "And I wasn't *mooning over him.*"

"Absolutely you were." Jewel snickered. "You had it bad."

"No," she corrected, "I was a little desperate for a rescue, but I wasn't acting like it."

"I wonder," she muttered. "It'd be interesting to see how he feels about you."

"He doesn't even know me." She glared at Jewel. "Please

don't make things awkward while we're here."

"No, I won't." Jewel waved her hand. "I shouldn't even tease you, but it makes me feel better so …"

"Hey, anything right now to make us feel better is worth gold." Nellie smiled in understanding. "But I really don't want something like that to be brought up, especially not in front of him."

"No, I understand that. God, we're all such a mess, aren't we? I just want my daughter back."

"Come on. Let's go see if there's coffee."

At that, Jewel stared at her. "Like *coffee*, coffee?" Then she shook her head. "God, I sound weird even to me."

"I don't know for sure if there's coffee, but maybe we can get some. Come on. Let's go find out."

"You know I'd kill for a cup of coffee."

Nellie winced at the phrase but ignored it. When they walked into the living room, Aiden was pouring four cups. "Oh, good Lord," she murmured. "I was really hoping for coffee, but I wasn't really expecting it."

He looked over, smiled. "Hey, we aim to please."

"You saved us already. It's hard enough for us to ask for anything more."

"On the other hand," Jewel said, "I'll ask, and, if it's a no, then it's a no."

Aiden looked at her. "What can you use?"

"You mean, outside of rescuing my daughter and the other women and children? I need food," she said bluntly, "clothes, more food, and a shower. Maybe after that we'll have some idea how to get this nightmare behind me, and that'll only happen if I can get my daughter back safe."

"And you said that the kidnappers had found a home for your daughter to go to?"

She nodded. "They're selling the kids," she stated bluntly, "and I think somebody requested a newborn." She sent a sideways glance over at Nellie.

Nellie felt the color sucked out of her cheeks. "Well, they're not getting mine."

"No, they won't," Corbin confirmed, coming up and wrapping an arm around her shoulders, tugging her gently to him. "I promise you that."

She stared up at him, feeling the same sense of security and relief when she had seen him for the first time. "Please promise me that, whatever happens …"

He nodded immediately. "I have no problem promising that. They aren't getting the baby." And he gently patted her tummy.

She wrapped her arms around him and murmured, "I'm not supposed to have very much coffee, but I could really use that cup."

"A couple cups a day probably are not an issue, and sometimes—well—nothing will do the job but coffee."

She nodded. "Absolutely."

He nudged her toward the dining table. "Sit down and relax. You need to take a load off those feet of yours."

She smiled. "These feet have been through a lot already, but I will survive."

"But they didn't hurt you, right?"

"No, not at all." Nellie looked over at Jewel. "In fact, they treated me probably better than anybody."

"That they did," Jewel confirmed. "It was a bone of contention for me at first, but I quickly realized that they were trying to keep her pregnancy healthy."

"Which, if they already had a buyer for the baby, would make sense," Aiden agreed.

Nellie immediately reached her hand down and gently stroked her belly. "It's okay, sweetheart."

Corbin looked at her. "Any idea what it is? Boy or girl?"

She shook her head. "No, I didn't want to know, as I don't care. As long as my baby is healthy, I'm good. Surprises in this instance are a good thing."

He placed a cup of coffee in front of her. "Now we only have dry goods here. We can order you something in a little bit, but, if you're really hungry," he noted, "there's bread in the freezer. We can make toast for you."

"That's a start." She looked over at Jewel for her input, then back to Corbin. "Is there any canned tuna?"

He nodded. "Yep, if that's what you want."

"It's a start." But something was off with him. She eyed him carefully and asked, "What are you not telling us?"

"Let's just say that the group has disappeared. I haven't received a full report yet, so I can't say more than that for now."

"Of course they've disappeared," she murmured, as she looked over at Jewel, who'd shoved her hand to her mouth to stop from crying out. Nellie immediately reached out a hand to Jewel. "Wait until we get more news. It doesn't have to be bad news."

"I know that some people have been rescued," Corbin shared, "but I've held off telling you until I know exactly who and what we know so far."

"Children?" Jewel asked quietly.

"*Some* children. I don't know who it is yet," he repeated, with a warning look.

And Nellie looked over at Jewel to see her sitting there, her eyes stricken. Nellie nodded. "Then we'll wait and see." She gripped Jewel's hand in hers. "We came this far. Let's stay strong."

As days went, this one had a better middle part than it had started out. Now if only they could end the day by pulling a few more miracles from the hat.

CORBIN STUDIED THE two women, the one he was quite impressed with and the other one—obviously much more traumatized and had been a prisoner for much longer. After he gave Jewel a cup of coffee and put the toast on, he studied Nellie. "Healthwise you seem okay. Were you given any injections?"

She frowned at that. "I don't know. Maybe at the beginning, but I seem to have been okay afterward. I didn't cause any trouble. I just thanked them politely for the food and the water that I was given. Originally I was drugged, starting with the kidnapping, and then later with the food, I think. That seemed to ease off." She hesitated, then added, "I think one of the men may have helped us to escape."

At that, Aiden turned and looked at her in surprise. "Can you describe him?"

She looked at him and asked, "What difference does it make?"

"Because, if an ally is inside, we would want to go easier on him."

Immediately she said, "He's tall. Maybe early thirties, red hair, curly mostly. Caring."

"So what's he doing with that group then?" Jewel snapped. "He treated me like an asshole."

"Did he ever hit you? Did he ever hurt you?" Nellie asked Jewel.

Jewel frowned and then shrugged. "Honestly I don't remember if it was him or the other guy."

"The other guy"—Nellie looked back at Corbin—"he's big, maybe six-two. ... Rough, you know? Kind of a body-builder, but he doesn't seem to have the muscle definition. He's just big."

He nodded. "And that happens if somebody stops going to the gym on a regular basis."

"Right. He's mostly bald. He's a little bit older, maybe late thirties, early forties."

"Any recognition or resemblance between the two?"

She stared at him in surprise, looked over at Jewel, and slowly shook her head. "Not that I could see. If you're asking if they were brothers or cousins or something, I couldn't really tell."

As he thought about it, Corbin looked over at Nellie. "Did you ever hear the two men interact?"

"Yes, at least at the end. The second guy, that meaner older guy, came around and didn't come out and say anything clearly, but it was implied that the younger man wouldn't be allowed to make my life any easier."

"Do you feel like that good guy was still there, or did they do something to him?"

"I don't think they did something to him right after I overheard that conversation because I think he's the one who opened the door and let us out. Whether he'd already been threatened, and that was his way of reacting, I don't know."

Corbin nodded. "We see all kinds of relationships on both sides of the law. Some that bond through killing. Some bond through blackmail. Some bond by sticking it to the one person in question. All kinds of people are out there who are absolute shits on the inside." Corbin had seen a lot of them. But it made him wonder not only what was the relationship with these two men and what would it have taken for this guard to have let them go free.

She quickly explained about the door being obviously unlocked.

"So a passive move," Corbin noted.

"Which," Nellie added, "if he thought he would get caught, then even that move was taking a big chance."

Corbin nodded at that too. "Any chance you could work with a sketch artist?"

She stared at him. "I think so, yes." She looked over at Jewel. "What about you?"

Jewel huffed. "Absolutely. I'll see their faces in my nightmares for years."

Corbin reached for his phone. "I'll get one in."

"You can just do that?" Jewel asked, frowning at him.

He smiled. "We can get anything we need."

"Well, I *need* fried chicken," Jewel said immediately.

He stared at her in astonishment. "Okay then, that'll be next."

She returned his stare, then her gaze narrowed. "Are you just teasing me?"

"No, you want fried chicken, and you can have fried chicken," he stated simply. "I was planning to ask you what you want for lunch anyway."

"Are we staying?" she asked. "I thought we were potentially moving."

"Potentially, yes, but, so far, Aiden hasn't found any sign that our location has been compromised."

"So we're safe here?" she asked.

He nodded and smiled. "Yes, we're safe. For the moment. Until I hear otherwise."

"I would like to call my father," Nellie whispered. "Hopefully today."

"Absolutely today." Jewel glared at Corbin. "Do you think we got out of one captivity to turn around and be captives again?"

At that, he slowly turned and looked at her. "You're not a captive. The door is right there. Feel free to walk." She frowned at him, and he frowned right back.

"So why are we here?" Jewel snapped.

"Because we want to make sure that we weren't followed getting here. You don't remember, but an awful lot of bullets were flying during our retreat."

"Sure, but you also said nobody found us, so why isn't there a full contingent of police here to get us out?"

"We can call them, if that's what you want." He tilted his head to the side. "As long as you're 100 percent sure that the kidnappers are not coming after you. Remember. They may not have been physically following us in another vehicle to this location, yet they could have tracked us via air."

At that, Nellie smiled. "I'd like to stay here."

He nodded approvingly. "Good decision."

But Jewel was not deterred. "There's absolutely no reason for the kidnappers to come after us."

"Sure there is," Nellie replied instantly. "We can identify both of them. Why do you think Corbin wants to bring in an artist?"

"So, if that sketch artist is with the cops, then they'll protect us too?"

"Yeah, like the cops found us before." Nellie stared Jewel. "How long have those women been there?"

"I don't know," Jewel answered slowly. "I've been there just over two months, ... I think."

"Right, and the cops didn't find you in that time frame. Would you trust them to keep you safe now?"

At that, Jewel frowned. "I want my daughter."

"And that's another reason why I want you here. Our teams need to go in and to get the last of the captives out safely and to take down the men involved, so they don't set up shop somewhere else."

"And yet you haven't done that?"

"A search of the premises is in progress, plus a hunt is on for those who left."

"What did you mean earlier, when you said, *via air*?"

"Satellite. Street cams," he said simply. "You saw only two men, but I'm not sure that's all who were there or who are involved in this enterprise."

"No, there should be more involved," Nellie agreed. "It's too sophisticated for only two men, especially those two."

"Exactly, and we don't want to get just those two. We want to get everybody in charge, and we want to free the women and children."

"Can't you just free the women and children and go for the men afterward?" Jewel asked anxiously.

"We did that and managed to free several, as I told you, but they have gone back in for another look. That building is empty, but we think a second building might be connected to these guys. We need access to see if anyone is there."

"And then what?" she asked and stared at him intently. "Those who escaped, can you track them?"

"Yes." He nodded. "A team is being pulled together now."

"Including the cops?"

"Yes. Aiden and I work underground. We do the job that's needed to be done, and the local PDs get the glory."

"Isn't that what the FBI is supposed to do?"

"Probably, but we operate with a whole lot fewer rules and a whole lot more autonomy, and honestly our system works a hell of a lot better. Besides, there's no FBI here in England."

"Until my daughter is in my arms, I won't believe anything."

"I don't blame you," he said cheerfully.

Just then came a knock on the door. He held a finger to his lips as he walked over, put his ear against the door, and then made a series of tapping sounds. When it was answered on the other side, he opened the door and let in a stranger. "Hi, I'm Corbin."

"I'm Mitch, sketch artist," the young man replied. "Where's the person I need to talk to?"

"There are two of them." And Corbin led Mitch into the kitchen and introduced the two women. "This is Mitch, the sketch artist."

At that, Nellie straightened. "That was fast."

"That's what happens when you have resources," Corbin explained. "Now let's get an image of these guys as fast as we can." At that, he walked over, poured himself a second cup of coffee and one for the sketch artist, adding, "I'll be in the other room, getting logistics together. If you need me, you know where I am." And, with that, he walked out, Aiden at his aside. Once on the couch, he asked, "Any update?"

"It's all quiet at the initial warehouse."

"Do you think they're still there? I don't. I imagine they have a second location to lay low, while they figure out what the fallout will be. And those who left before, have they returned?"

"No way to know," Aiden noted. "I'm sure the bad guys

are putting plans in place, just in case. Surely they have a second warehouse or the likes."

"Exactly, and I imagine they'll move fast. We got one woman and two kids out of the initial warehouse, didn't we?" Aiden nodded. "I'm considering going in there tonight to make a final sweep—maybe we'll unearth their alternate location by that time too."

"Not alone," Aiden snapped. "I'll come with you."

"What about the women?"

"They should be safe here, if we leave them locked up."

"They won't like that. Hell, I don't like it. We need security for them."

"Maybe they won't be safe, but, if they know we're going after the children, they might be okay with it. You can't go in alone. There are too many variables."

"Yeah, both of us going would be the best." And, with that, Corbin brought up his laptop and ordered security for the two women. He checked his watch and asked Aiden, "Time frame?"

"I would give it another two hours, then move. I'd like to get there before the cops' planned raid."

With that, Corbin glanced toward the kitchen. "The sketches need to be done first."

"I don't know if he can be done that fast."

"No, that's a good point. Why don't you go see how they're doing?"

Aiden got up, walked into the kitchen, grabbed a coffee, while Corbin watched. Aiden came back out. "They're doing pretty well."

"Good, so maybe two hours would be fine." He confirmed the time frame for the security and then ordered copies of the satellite feed. As soon as that came through, he brought it up and started searching the kidnappers' warehouse. "We need blueprints." He added that into the request for the team. It took another few minutes for that to show up. After he had that, he requested security camera access to the intersection at the one corner adjacent that building.

"Do you think the kidnappers will be coming through that intersection?"

"Somebody will have. They might remember to change up their route a time or two, but these guys? I doubt they would remember every time."

"Good point."

Corbin pondered the video feed.

"You know the cops will want to go in first," Aiden suggested.

"Yeah, well, we can tell them about it, but we're going in ahead of their time frame."

"How much time ahead?"

"Why don't you tell them to come in two hours after us? Put them on alert for earlier. We'll let them know how it goes."

And, with Aiden working in the background to set that up, Corbin studied the blueprints and the city camera feeds at the intersection for just the last week, since Corbin and Aiden were on a tight schedule. One vehicle Corbin saw partially on a regular basis. But it always stayed just out of the camera's field of vision. Until one time when somebody else parked at the front of the warehouse, so he had to go around, closer to the sidewalks, and, at that point, the camera caught a better picture of his vehicle.

"Bingo," Corbin whispered. He quickly punched the make, the model, and the license plate into the Mavericks' Chat window. When it came back later, he froze. "Now that would be stupid." He got up, disconnected his laptop, walked into the kitchen, and held up the screen to Nellie. "Is this him?"

She stared at the picture, and her eyes widened, and she nodded immediately. "Yes, yes."

He turned his laptop to Jewel, who nodded too. "Yeah, that's the one who was nice to her."

Corbin turned toward the sketch artist, who nodded when he got a look at the face on the laptop screen.

"Good," Mitch said, "then we only have the other sketch to do."

"We'll work on this guy," Corbin stated. "You guys keep working on that other guard." And he turned, headed back to do his laptop work in the living room. He looked up to Aiden. "This is the guy who helped the women escape. Tell the local authorities too. We need a full rundown on who this guy is, his known associates. They're trying to get a sketch of the second guard right now."

"Good." Aiden grinned. "Even getting this much is huge."

"Yes, this is the break we needed. Now we must pick up this guy." Just as he went to make a phone call, Corbin's phone rang.

"We ID'd your guy with facial recognition pinging his DL. One *Frankie Taylor*. However, this guy has no record, not even a speeding ticket," Hatch said, without preamble, "not registered with any kind of school, university, or any educational institutes. And I checked US and UK databases. What's worse, he has no business affiliates, so it's pretty hard to find anything about him."

"And that's likely why he was picked for this. He kept a very low profile." Corbin sighed. "We need a list of all family, including cousins and best friends, everyone in his circle."

"Well, he has no social media presence, so that narrows that down."

"I suspect that he has some kind of relationship with the second guard, who wasn't quite so friendly," Corbin shared. "I'm not sure just what kind of a relationship though."

"How friendly was this guy?" Hatch asked.

"The women think Frankie left the door deliberately unlocked, so the women could escape. And they took advantage of it and left the building, so we could scoop them up, while we were peppered with bullets—which could also mean this Frankie guy is no longer on this planet."

"It's possible, but only if they suspect it was him who set the women free. If he made it look like the other guard did it, … who knows? If he made it look like an accident, well, I mean an accident might be forgivable, but, if they lost two assets, chances are he's done for anyway."

"I was wondering that too," Corbin noted.

"We'll check the morgue." With that, Hatch rang off, with a long list of things to be checked.

Corbin studied the blueprints of this big warehouse, where Nellie and Jewel had been held. Much of it steel and concrete. It was also a fairly isolated large building on a big commercial lot, which worked to the kidnappers' favor. Nobody was close by to hear screaming. There was easy access, and the kidnappers could bring their victims into the warehouse and out again, without being easily seen.

Corbin stared at the blueprints, shook his head, and muttered, "Assholes."

CHAPTER 8

M ITCH WAS A professional, and the sketch was coming along nicely. Jewel had a lot stronger memories, so everything she brought up, Nellie usually agreed with. In half an hour, they stared at a really decent sketch, and Nellie felt shivers going down her spine. She looked over at the artist. "That's him," she whispered.

Jewel got up from beside her and turned and walked away, but not before Nellie heard her friend's sobs. Nellie looked over at the artist and whispered, "Thank you."

He nodded quietly. "I'm sorry."

"Let's hope we can get this solved now."

He got up, collected all his stuff to leave. At that moment in time, Corbin walked in, took one look, and asked, "Is it close?"

"It's very close, as in scary close," Nellie replied.

"Good. I hate to say that that's a good thing, but, in this case, the closer we can get to IDs for your two jailers, the better chance we have of locating them." He looked at the artist and asked, "Do you have a way to scan it?"

The artist nodded. "Yes." He did something with his phone. Next thing she knew, he was packing up again.

She looked over at Corbin. "Now what?"

"Now all kinds of stuff. For one, our artist here is leaving, and your chicken is on its way." He looked at Jewel.

She stared at him. "You know that I'd rather have so many more important things than chicken."

"Doesn't matter. If chicken makes one of you happy right now, then we're happy. Obviously the rest is in progress, and we're doing everything we can." She had to appreciate that because he was right here for her, with anything that could help ease Jewel's mind right now.

Nellie noted Corbin had his jacket on. Her heart sagged. "Are you leaving?"

He nodded, and she swallowed hard and whispered, "Do you have to?"

"No, I don't have to, but it's best if I do."

She frowned at that. "Why?"

"Because I'm going back to the building where you were held to see where the kids are, before the police do their raid."

She stared at him in horror. "Why you?"

His lips twitched. "Because that's what I do."

She glared at him. "Aren't you supposed to look after us?" Nellie didn't know why she felt so contrary, but the fact that he was leaving just sent her nerves into overdrive. "I don't feel safe with you gone," she finally whispered uncomfortably.

"I get that, but you will be safe here."

She looked over at Aiden. "It's nothing against you, Aiden."

"Good, because I'm leaving too." And he flashed a big grin at her.

She gasped in horror. "Really? What about us then?"

"You will have a full-time security guard," Corbin said, his voice calm. "You will be fine. We will be back within two hours."

"Or," Aiden smiled, "we'll contact you within two hours."

"What's with that two-hour time frame?"

"We have police coming as backup at that point, so, for what it's worth, there should definitely be some movement by then."

She stared at him in horror. "You guys are going in alone? These guys are out to kill. ... You know that, right?"

"Yeah, we do know that," Corbin confirmed. "We're also after Jewel's daughter, and you don't want us to miss her, do you?"

Of course not, and she felt like a fool for even protesting this much. "No, of course not." But she still glared at him. "And that's dirty pool."

"What is?" he asked.

But from the twitch of his lips, she knew he understood. She crossed her arms over her chest. "I don't like it."

"Noted. I'll take it under consideration, but we can't change it now. We have to move, and we have to move now."

At that, she realized the artist was already gone, and the door was closing behind him. "What about information on this second guy? Don't you want background information on him first?"

"Our team is searching for him right now," he replied quietly. "We will find him, if he's out there."

"Oh, he's out there," she snapped. "Probably causing more chaos with every step he takes."

"Guys like this do," he murmured. "Not to worry. We will let you know what happens."

"Are you coming back here?" And again she couldn't understand why, but the fact that he was leaving sent her nerves on edge. She wrapped her arms around her chest to ward off the sudden chill.

He walked over, grabbed her by the shoulders, and said in a very quiet voice, "You will be fine. Nobody will get you guys here. The security guard is outside, and I promise we will be back."

"I don't really have a choice anyway, do I?" She glared up at him.

"No," he said equally firmly. "You don't." And, with that, he added, "Now either I can give you a hug or I can leave without one. Which would you prefer?"

She stared up at him, wanting desperately to say, *No hug,* and to tell him to take off and to get lost—at the same time, she didn't know why, but she felt like she desperately needed that hug. He opened his arms, and she walked into them, burying her face against his chest. "You be careful," she whispered.

He just held her for a long moment, then released her, as he stepped back and smiled. "Now you two be good."

She snorted at that. "Why do I have to be good? After what I've been through, I should be able to kick up my heels."

He grinned. "Hold that thought. I promise I'll be back."

"You can't promise that."

"Yes, I can promise to do my best to return. And, while we are gone, no phone calls, no nothing until we get back."

"What about my father?"

"He has been notified that you've been found. Nothing else has been said to him, except that you're alive."

She sighed. "Well, at least that's something."

"It is, indeed. He is clamoring to see you, so we won't hold him off for long."

"I still don't quite understand why you're trying to hold him off."

"Because all communications could endanger you. Until we have these guys in custody," he explained quietly, "it's all about keeping you safe."

She shivered, but she couldn't argue with them. She watched, her heart heavy, as he walked out the door. With the door open, she saw the guard standing there, talking with him. It was such an odd feeling to think that they had a guard, but, at the same time, she knew she was supposed to be grateful because it would help them. One way or the other, it would be to their benefit.

All she wanted was Corbin back, safe and sound. When the door closed with a finality, she couldn't argue further, as she turned and headed to the kitchen to the coffeepot. And then she got a whiff of the aroma coming from the bag on the table. She called out to Jewel. When she didn't answer, Nellie walked into the bedroom to find Jewel lying on the bed, curled up in a fetal position.

Nellie walked over, dropped down beside her, and picked up her hand. "I know you don't want food, but right now the men are gone. We're on our own, except for the guard outside, and anything we can do to keep up our spirits is important."

Jewel just stared at her, dry-eyed. "I just don't care. All I want is my daughter back."

"They've gone to get her, and I know that probably doesn't make you feel any better, but they have gone to see if they can find her."

She stared at her hopefully. "Do you think they'll succeed?"

"These guys? A definite yes," she said, with conviction.

"I don't think very much gets in their way."

Jewel smiled at that. "Well, you have been right so far. I guess it won't hurt to stand by your optimism a little bit longer."

"Nope, it sure won't. Remember. When your daughter gets here, you need to be in much better shape than you're in now."

She snorted that. "I don't think my daughter would have any trouble with me. No matter what way I am."

"No, and I agree with you there." Nellie rose. "Come on. We've got fried chicken, and, while we're eating, you can tell me why you asked for fried chicken, when we could have asked for the world."

At that, Jewel gave her a teary smile. "It brings back memories of my happy childhood." She slowly stood. "My brother worked in a fried chicken restaurant, and every morning I would race downstairs, hoping against hope that he brought leftovers home. More often than not he had, and we would sit there in the morning and happily eat them." She gave a bright smile. "Memories of a happier time."

"You know something? That's a hell of a good reason to enjoy fried chicken. Come on. Let's go try it out." With that, the two women headed to the kitchen.

TWO BLOCKS AWAY from the kidnappers' warehouse, Corbin quickly loaded up his weapons and prepped for what lay ahead.

Aiden looked at him and smiled. "This life suits you."

"Maybe, but I was also thinking that maybe it was time to get out."

"I think we all wonder that."

"Even you?" Corbin asked his friend.

"Absolutely." Aiden laughed. "I like how there's one un-attached captive, and she turns to you."

"Jewel is single," he replied.

"Jewel is a different case. She doesn't want anybody right now, except for her daughter back," he murmured. "I was talking about Nellie, and you know it."

He laughed. "Yeah, I absolutely do know it. She's pretty special."

"Have you noticed how she turns to you each and every time?"

"I can definitely see that an attraction is there. I mean, hell, I'm human, so why wouldn't I?"

"Of course." Aiden gave an eye roll. "You're human, so why wouldn't there be but …" He grinned at his friend. "It is interesting to note how much she has responded to you though."

"Maybe," Corbin replied cautiously. "Regardless of how she's responding, she's in shock. She's just been through a hell of an ordeal, and let's not forget that she's pregnant."

"And I think I heard something about problems with her father, but I don't know what it was."

Corbin nodded. "Let's get this show happening. There'll be time for tying ups bits and pieces afterward."

"If you say so. But I think it would impact your chances. I mean, obviously if she's got a partner waiting in the wings …"

"I'm assuming she does, unless some asshole just dumped her. Yet she's not really the kind who an asshole would dump."

"According to these women, all kinds of men do shit like

that." Aiden exited the vehicle, closing the door silently. "I can't say it's ever been my particular system, but hey ..."

"No, but you know something? In all the years that we've been doing this work, none of us have ever had a long-term relationship."

"I know, and of course we understand the reason for that too."

"Absolutely. Our careers are hard on everybody."

"Is that another reason why you're looking to get out?"

"It's just one of the questions I was pondering. You want something else in life, then you have to make a change. And, in this case, to support the kind of lifestyle I want after-ward? ... Well, of course, we're getting well paid to work for the Mavericks."

"We are," Aiden confirmed.

"The question is though, are we getting paid enough to retire soon, with the money we sock away?"

"I don't know. I guess it depends on what happens at the end of this op to the Mavericks. Do we have any more ops after this one?"

"I pretty well have enough to retire already, not that I'll stop working, but I might change things up. Yet I have to admit—when a chance to go out on an op and something like this comes up—it's not hard to accept."

"No, it sure isn't. So it's something that we'll just have to keep in mind."

Corbin nodded. As they were all geared up, he said, "Check in every ten minutes."

"Got it." Aiden grinned. "Just like old times." He head-ed to the right, while Corbin took off to the left.

Corbin watched his friend leave, hoping that this would not be the last Mavericks mission he was part of, where he had to say goodbye to somebody he trusted and cared about. The two of them went way back, but the Mavericks had partnered them up again. However, Corbin also knew that things went wrong plenty of times in life. He called out, his voice low and soft, "Watch your back."

Aiden lifted a hand and murmured, "Always."

As Corbin was about to head in his direction, Hatch texted him.

We've got an address for the one guard. We've got the second guard's face going through facial recognition right now.

Good luck with that, and we'll talk to you in two hours or less. And then Corbin shut down communications and went dark. It was one of the precautions that they always followed on missions to block any access of the enemy.

Did these guys know enough about how to track other phone calls?

Did they have technology that would allow them to see an approach coming?

Did they have heat-sig cameras out here?

What else did they possibly have which would put him and Aiden in danger?

Corbin believed the devil was in details because he had been serious about possibly retiring. He could. He was wondering about setting up a training center for people like him. Or even for law enforcement because he'd worked with a lot of them too.

But those were all ideas milling in the back of his brain. His agreement with the Mavericks was to do this job and potentially no more. Although Corbin understood, if he did this job, he would then be helping Aiden on the next. And that would be fine with Corbin. He wouldn't want just anybody else watching Aiden's back.

Corbin hoped that he could convince his friend to retire with him, and they could settle down and maybe go into business together.

He smiled at that idea because he didn't know the first thing about horses. So maybe not horses. Maybe dogs. He loved dogs, but he had to get through this job, and he had to find a reason to not accept the next. With that, his thoughts immediately went to Nellie. And back to the job at hand.

The darkness was all-encompassing at this hour of the night. It helped that a storm converged above and that the north wind was coming in fast and hard. It would also make it easier when he shut down the power inside. The storm would get blamed, unless these guys were watching out for them, in which case, ... *well, all bets were off.*

He smiled at that because that was his way of doing things. *All bets off* was the best way in the world. You had to be prepared for everything, and he hoped that these guys wouldn't be prepared in the least. Not everybody who pulled a con like this had any idea what to do when shit hit the fan.

Although, if the kidnappers were smart, they'd be a long way away by now.

Corbin had to ensure that he took out the main players, and then law enforcement would pick up everyone else. There was always a chance of missing somebody. It was a fact of life that shit happened, and you did the best that you could but no way to guarantee that the good guys would get every one of the bad guys involved.

As Corbin slipped along the outer wall to the power meter, he quickly cut the electricity to the building. He waited to see if anybody came out. Worst case scenario for Corbin was that he and Aiden got more captives out but none of the men responsible for kidnapping them. He wanted the perpetrators of this, so they couldn't do this again.

If he found just a couple kids, Corbin could snag them and run. But if half a dozen toddlers were inside, that would make this a whole lot more difficult. He couldn't even imagine the logistics of setting up something like this on short notice. Did the children come first, and then they found buyers; or did they have buyers, and then they go looking for children?

His mind also went to motive. Did it start small and then snowball on them, as people put in requests for newborns—like in the case of Nellie. With Nellie back in his mind again, all Corbin could think about was who was the father to her child.

Where was he? Because no way in hell, if Corbin's girl-friend were pregnant, would he have left her to deal with life all on her own. But he also knew a lot of people would. If they didn't like what was happening, they would just walk.

With the outside parking lights shut off, and the entire area in darkness, Corbin moved swiftly forward. He hadn't heard from Aiden, but then he didn't expect to for another few minutes.

Right on target, he got an owl call out in the middle of the night. Corbin answered it with a call of his own. He had learned to throw his voice a long time ago to make it sound like he was off in a different direction. It came in handy at times like this. Who knew a childhood game could become a lifesaving skill?

He came to the front door, quickly disengaged the lock, and slipped inside. He waited just a hair of a moment for his eyes to adjust and flicked on his night vision goggles and started searching the main room.

135

It was set up into multiple rooms, with a hallway down the center. He frowned at that because it was almost like a series of bedrooms. Perfect for housing kidnapped kids. But it was so silent inside. Was anyone even here?

As he moved through the rooms, he found them all empty. So this trip was a waste of time. Corbin was getting more and more concerned, until Aiden sent him a signal, code for *he'd found something.*

At that, Corbin swept through the next few rooms and then reached the stairs going up. When his phone vibrated, he looked down at the incoming text. Aiden had found two children—a boy and a girl. He was upstairs at the back north corner.

With that intel, Corbin quickly picked up the pace, searched all the remaining rooms down on his level and headed upstairs. As long as Aiden had two children, he couldn't leave them to keep looking. And Corbin would like to search the entire building before he got to Aiden.

By the time Corbin got to the far end, with still more rooms to check, Aiden popped his head around the door and whispered, "I haven't checked any of these next six rooms."

"And the children?"

"They're asleep. … Possibly drugged."

"Drugs would make sense. Send Hatch photos."

"Already done. We'll need medics for them."

"I just don't understand why nobody's here."

"Because the children are drugged, I would imagine."

Corbin nodded and quickly checked the next four rooms. With only two more to go, he opened one, and his heart sank against his chest. A child's bed was in the corner and contained two occupants. He crept closer and realized it was two little girls. Hoping against hope that one of these was Jewel's daughter, he quickly snapped a photo, even while he checked for a pulse on each girl.

They were sleeping, but it was a very deep sound sleep. If the others were drugged, then these little girls would be too.

At the next door, gun at the ready, he opened it and stepped inside. He heard a breath, but it was slow and labored. With his goggles on, Corbin saw a large man collapsed on the floor. He raced over to the man, quickly checked for a pulse, and, from the pooling blood underneath him, knew he was badly injured. It was Frankie. Corbin gave him a hard shake. "What happened?"

Frankie groaned, obviously in pain.

"You need to tell me what happened."

"He shot me."

"Who shot you?"

"My asshole partner. I was trying to talk him out of selling these kids, but the money was too good, and he wouldn't listen."

"Of course it was. Are you the one who let the women go?"

Frankie stared at him in shock and then slowly gasped. "Did they make it?"

"They did. That's why we're here now."

Frankie sagged back again. "Thank God for that."

"What can you tell me about your partner?"

"He'll kill you as soon as he sees you."

"No one's here."

"He'll be back."

"How do you know?"

"Because he's coming back to finish me off. He just shot me and left me here to suffer."

"That shot would eventually kill you anyway."

"You need to get the kids out. Fast. He's coming back with reinforcements."

At that, Corbin stared at him. "And what about you?"

"Get the kids out. I deserve whatever happens to me for these kids and for that poor woman."

"The one you killed, Mary?"

"I don't know who she was. And I didn't kill her. I only found out afterward. I knew my days were numbered at that point."

"We have the body of Mary Hennessy."

"That could be her. I don't think I ever knew her name."

"Yet you started down this pathway."

Frankie waved his hand weakly. "I know. I know. The only good thing is, I got no parents or family to give a shit, when they find out what I've done."

"No, that might be true," Corbin said, "but I don't know that you'll make it through this."

"Probably not." Frankie gasped once more. "So, if there's justice in this world or the next, I'll have to face it on the other side." He coughed once and then again. "*Goooo*, don't waste time with me. Get them out. He'll come back soon."

"How many children are here?"

"There's five now. I moved five here to this adjacent location."

With his heart sinking, Corbin said, "I only found four."

Frankie's eyes opened wide, and he stared at Corbin. "He's doing the delivery right now, ... that little girl."

"Do you know where the delivery is going down?" Corbin asked urgently. "We have to stop it before it happens."

Frankie took a breath and then another. "He said it's on Grundle."

"Grundle what?"

"Grundle Road. No, Grundle Highway," he murmured. "Can't remember."

"What vehicle is he driving?" Corbin had Hatch on the line, as he quickly pulled up his phone and had the injured guard repeat the information.

"It's a big warehouse."

"What kind of a warehouse?"

"It's a shipping import-export warehouse. They bring clothing in from China." And he gave the company name, but Corbin couldn't understand, so he asked Hatch to hang on, so Frankie could spell that. He had started to choke again.

"Did he say Xiao Exports?" Hatch asked, his voice calm on the other side.

"That's as close as I could hear. What have you got?"

"Two units heading toward the warehouse right now, plus ambulances. But I'm not exactly sure that we'll be in time to stop the exchange."

"Depends how much lead time he has on us." He looked down at the dying man. "Do you know when he left?"

Frankie shook his head. "No," he whispered. "He's cagey, and he won't be taken alive. That I am sure of."

"I don't give a shit if he gets killed in this, but I've got an injured mother, who's terrified about her daughter."

"Yes. Jewel," the guard said. "She'll be devastated."

"She *is* devastated. There's no *will* about it," Corbin snapped. "How the hell did you think this was a good idea?"

"Drunk," he whispered painfully, "drunk and high. My buddy set it up, and I took part in it. I didn't even really realize that they were killing the mothers. Seriously I didn't, not until afterward. Then, when I tried to get out of it, there was no going back."

"How many were involved?"

"Four. My buddy and I as their guards and the two sellers, who arranged the buyouts. And some kid scout, who searched for the women, but I don't think they are using him anymore. The sellers are at the warehouse too for the exchange."

"Good, with any luck we'll catch them all."

"Not likely," he whispered. "They're too smart. Been doing this kind of shit for a long time."

"How did your friend get into this?" he asked, staring down at his phone, waiting for Hatch to give him some information.

"I don't know."

"How did you two meet up?"

"Jail."

"Isn't that always the case. You come with ideas on how to make more money. Nobody ever wants to go straight. They just want to make fast money, and they don't even think about the consequences."

"I just wanted drugs," Frankie whispered. "It was always the drugs with me." Then he coughed once, twice, and fell silent afterward.

Corbin checked for a pulse, but there was nothing. This guy was gone. Into his phone, Corbin barked at Hatch, "I need an address for the exporters, and we need it now. Also get medics here at the warehouse. We've got four children, all drugged, and we've got one child in the middle of a buy going down at the exporter's warehouse."

Just then he got another phone call coming in. "I've got

to go, Hatch."

As soon as he answered the other call, it was Nellie, her voice tremulous. "Corbin," she screamed. "Your security guard is dead."

He swore into the phone, and then another voice came on the phone. "I hear you're looking for me, asshole. You know women can produce kids all the damn time—for instance, this bitch. Although this one is more of a problem, so I'll just pop her one."

Corbin closed his eyes, swearing under his breath. "What do you want?'

"I know you want this one. I know you do from the way she spoke to you. You'll deal or else."

"No deal, unless you leave both women alone, and you return Jewel's daughter," Corbin roared. "You need to bring back the kid."

"Too damn bad. The kid is already sold."

And, with that, Jewel wailed in the background. Corbin heard her sob and scream. A shot rang out. "Serves the bitch, right."

Corbin stared into the phone. "Fuck," he roared, already racing to the vehicle.

"Yeah, well, you wanted a deal," the shooter snapped. "I wanna deal too, but now that she's off the table, so is her damn kid."

CHAPTER 9

N ELLIE STARED AT the gunman fearfully. There had been a hard *pop* earlier, and the next thing she knew, the door to their apartment had been pushed open, and here he was. "Why did you have to shoot Jewel?" she cried out, racing to her friend's side.

"The woman has been a pain in the ass since the beginning."

"You stole her child." She glared at him fiercely. "What did you expect she'd do?"

He shrugged. "I didn't really expect most women to give a shit. My sisters didn't. I mean, they'd cheerfully sold their kids. I should have just had them produce half a dozen."

"Maybe," she said. "But I can't imagine that that's something they would have wanted to do in the first place."

"For the kind of money I'm getting paid, hell, yeah. They would have sold their kids in a heartbeat," he snapped. "It's only do-gooders, like you, who seem to be determined to keep them."

"That's because we love them." Her heart slammed against her chest, as she put pressure on Jewel's side, where blood pumped out sluggishly.

"You'll get over it. I've seen women get over all kinds of shit. It's really not a big deal."

She just stared at him in horror. Jewel was still alive, but she was unconscious. The bullet had gone into her side, and she needed a doctor, but, with this asshole here, the chances weren't good. Except Corbin knew. He'd be here soon. She pressed her hand harder over the wound to slow the bleeding.

"Come on. We have to leave."

"I thought you wanted to make a bargain," she said in surprise.

"Yeah, well, the one bargaining chip is already damaged and too much trouble. And you? ... Well, he's not getting you."

Her heart sank, and she knew it was back to her unborn child. "You're talking about my baby."

"Yeah, sure as hell I am." He laughed. "The money I'm getting paid for that sucker will let me get away from here and set up a whole new life."

Shocked, she stared at him. "For one child?"

"Yeah." He looked at her for a moment. "I guess you probably wouldn't sell it to me, would you?"

"No," she said immediately.

"I didn't think so. That's too bad."

"You know a lot of women are out there ..."

"Yeah, probably." He nodded agreeably. "So, yeah, you're right. I'll try that after this. Because honestly? Dealing with you guys is a pain in the ass."

She stared at him. "Am I supposed to apologize or something?" She stared at him in disgust. "You ripped us out of our lives, held us captive, and you've stolen what's most important to us, and here you are, blaming us?"

"Whatever." He glared at her. "Come on. We need to get the hell out of here."

"Fine." She struggled to her feet, grateful that she'd had

some food. Like hell he'd give her food now. Jewel needed help. She had to trust in Corbin to get here in time to save Jewel. Nellie snatched a bottle of water off the counter, as she moved out.

He looked at her and nodded. "Smart. I probably won't have too much time to get fussy over the next little while."

"Where are we going?"

"Somewhere to hole up safe, until you have your baby."

She kept her shudder to herself, but it was damn hard. "You know that I've still got months to go, right?"

"Yeah, I do. Although there is talk about inducing you, when you are closer, so they can control the delivery."

She swallowed hard, as he dragged her down the hallway. She hated to leave Jewel behind, but Nellie really wasn't given a choice. "You could have let me at least bandage her wound."

"Or I could just pop her once more," he snapped, with a hard look at her.

Given the choice, she was okay to leave and to keep this asshole away from Jewel. "Did you kill our guard?"

"Unless he's got a hard head, I doubt he'll survive."

"So what's that now? … Three murders?"

"Once you've done one, it really doesn't make a difference. You'll get hit the same as if you killed multiple people. And they just get easier."

"Including your friend. What happened to him?"

"He got soft," he said in disgust. "And that, I didn't see coming. I'll blame you for that."

"Me? Why?"

"In a way, I shouldn't have had him look after you. He's always had a soft touch for pregnant women. He tried to get me to let you walk away, but that wasn't happening. I tried to explain to him how much the money would make a difference in our lives, but then I realized that, if he'll be a pain in the ass, the money would make that much more of a difference in my life if I didn't have to split it."

"So you shot him?"

"Yeah, I did." He sneered. "And you know something? I think he saw it coming."

"Of course he did," she said quietly. "I'm sorry. He at least seemed to have some compassion."

"Like that'll get him far in life," he snapped.

"How did you guys even meet?"

"In jail. He was a junkie and a dealer. I just brought him up to the big players' world."

"What about the babies?"

"I'll go get them tomorrow, but not until I get you locked up somewhere safe."

She shook her head at that. "Or you could just let me go."

He laughed at her. "That is not happening. Believe me. So don't waste your breath on it."

She subsided, not wanting to piss him off. He was the kind of guy who would take her down, if he thought that she was playing games with him.

He looked at her and nodded. "Smart choice. I'm not soft, like Frankie. I'm not an asshole, but I'm not soft."

"No, and you have a plan."

"Exactly, you got to have a plan in life. It's losers who don't. Frankie was like that, and his plan was to get his next fix. Other than that he didn't give a crap. Look where that got him."

"Yeah, a one-way ticket to hell."

"Maybe, if hell is there, I'll deal with Frankie when it's

my number."

"You're prepared to die over something like this?" she asked curiously.

He frowned at her. "I ain't going to die."

"Well, the guys dealing with you, ... surely they must have a plan to not share profits too."

He stared at her for a long moment. "You're a pretty smart cookie," he murmured. "It is a possibility, isn't it?"

"It's a big possibility," she murmured. "Why would they share when you wouldn't?" It seemed like it was a really good time to shut up and to stay quiet, so she did.

He didn't say anything for a long moment, and then he swore. "Well, hell."

"What?" she murmured.

And then he thought about it some more. "No, they won't double-cross me right now. They need you."

"So what's to stop them from just taking me?" she asked quietly.

He looked at her in horror and then nodded. "That is something that they would do too." He frowned, his mind racing obviously. "I have to figure this out. I need time."

"And you will, just stay calm. Get part one of your plan down and then work on part two."

He laughed at that. "I can see why Frankie liked you."

"Hey, I'm easy to get along with," she muttered.

"Yeah, you've also got a brain in your head"—he grinned—"and that thing about working on part one, then part two? That's exactly what I will do."

She nodded. "Just don't be so rigid in your plans that you can't change them."

He looked at her and frowned. "What do you mean?"

"Something like this, like shooting your partner. Shooting Jewel. Killing Mary," she explained. "You got to be adaptable. Otherwise, when shit goes wrong, there's absolutely no way to adjust." By now they were at his vehicle, and he stuffed her into the front seat.

He nodded. "No, that's true. First, I got to make sure I'm safe. There's no point in having money if you can't spend it."

He drove in the darkness at a speed that made her very nervous. Several times she clutched the side handle.

"I'm a good driver. Don't worry about that."

"Maybe, but any kind of accident and of course ..." She put a hand to her belly.

"Right." And he groaned and slowed down. "I'm not used to thinking about anybody but myself."

"How's that worked out for you?" she murmured. "If you're trying to get a good payout, then you need to take a little bit better care of your cargo."

He snorted at that. "Or I could just drug you and keep you quiet the whole time."

She nodded. "Or you could do that. But, of course, then maybe me or the baby or both of us might not survive."

That shut him up. But she also knew that she was walking on thin ice with him. She wasn't sure how to get through to him and wasn't even sure it was possible. He had it in his head that this is what he would do, and she highly suspected that nobody would change his mind. She yawned.

He looked at her and nodded. "Yeah, you were always the one who slept the most."

"It's the pregnancy," she murmured.

"Well, it's good to know. Just in case I have to grab somebody else who's pregnant."

"I thought this case would set you up."

"It will, but I might need another one in order to set me up better."

She realized that he just wouldn't stop. No matter what happened to her, he would do this again and again. And her resolve deepened. "And you know that, the more times you do it, the more chances you have of getting caught."

"Yeah. Which is also why we have to make sure the payouts are good."

She couldn't imagine. "How can you even find people who want to pay for a child like this?"

"That's why the baby brokers are there."

"Oh, right. Those brokers who don't want to split the profits." He glared at her, and she shrugged. "It's what you said yourself."

"No, I said that *I* don't want to split the profits with Frankie."

"Well, you won't be doing that now. That's obvious. You killed him. Sure hope he wasn't a good friend."

At that, he was quiet for a moment. "Oh, he was."

"Wow," she muttered. "I guess you really don't understand what a friend is."

"No, *he* didn't," he snapped. "And he made my life a fucking nightmare now."

"Are you blaming him for that?" she asked curiously.

"Well, it is his fault. If he had just looked after you and not let you go ..."

"He didn't let us go." She stared at him, hoping to make him suffer—at least a little bit.

"What do you mean? The door was open."

"No, Jewel picked the lock." He stared at her in shock. "There was a nail inside our room. I don't know how she did it, but she picked the lock." At that, her captor started swearing a blue streak. "Is that why you killed your friend? ... Oh, my God."

He continued to glare at her. "I thought he left the door open for you."

She wouldn't let him get away with that, so she shook her head and lied. "No, Jewel picked the lock. And then we just booked it."

"Jesus Christ, and he told me that he was in the washroom and didn't know."

"That would explain why he wasn't there when we got out." Then she thought about and added, "Wow, you killed him for nothing. Well, no," she quickly amended, "you killed him because you didn't want to split the profits."

"Yeah, but I wouldn't have done that," he muttered, "if I knew that he hadn't let you go."

She didn't say anything. She just let that thought roll around in his brain, while he tried to figure things out now because that, in a way, changed everything. "When you thought you had been betrayed, you acted differently."

He started to swear, slamming his hand against the steering wheel, "Fuck, fuck, fuck," he roared.

She didn't say anything because what could she say? She knew the truth, but she wasn't telling him. Frankie deserved that much at least, and this asshole deserved to be haunted by the lie. She didn't even know why she felt a little bit of loyalty toward one of her captors, except he had made it possible for her to escape. When her current kidnapper fell silent, she looked over at him, but he was glaring into the window. Then she yawned again.

"Stop yawning."

She stared at him. "How am I supposed to do that?" she cried out in exasperation. "I'm pregnant. I need lots of sleep."

He sneered. "Women had been having babies for thousands of years. Do you think they got a chance to just sit down and rest?"

She stiffened at that. "Probably not, but they weren't being dragged around and starved either."

He looked over at her, frowned. "Didn't you get any food?"

"Not much," she lied. "Some toast is all there was. How did you find us there anyway?"

"I saw you guys go down that alley, so I waited," he murmured. "I was already trying to figure out how the hell you got loose in the first place. I had to go plug that leak, and I had the arrangement already for the baby, so I had to go deal with that," he muttered. "I figured that, as long as you guys were in one place, and you didn't know you'd been found, it was all good, and I could come back later. So it worked out for a change."

She nodded. "It did work out. At least for you."

He snorted. "Yeah, for me, and I don't give a shit about you."

"Got it," she muttered. "Message received. I'm just inventory that you're trying to keep safe."

"That's a good way to look at it. Yeah." He laughed. "You're inventory. An asset. That's that. Don't ever forget it, bitch."

As they came up to an intersection, quite a few other vehicles were around. When another vehicle came ripping up behind them, Nellie forced herself to not turn around, but her heart slammed with joy. It was Corbin. She knew it.

When her kidnapper pulled ahead through the intersection, Corbin came right up on his ass. Her kidnapper started swearing again. "What the hell does that fucker think he's doing?" He picked up speed. He looked over at her. "Hold on. Could be a bumpy ride."

She was already hanging on to the side of the door. She already knew what was coming. Corbin unleashed meant all kinds of shit would go down.

LEAVING AIDEN WITH the four kids and a team racing to Jewel's side, Corbin immediately picked up the trail from the satellite feed that Hatch had given him. Now Corbin saw the vehicle right ahead. He'd hauled ass to get here as fast as he could. But realizing a passenger was in the front seat and that she appeared to be sitting up, possibly okay, settled something inside him.

He didn't know when the hell he had started to care, beyond the fact that she was a job, but he did. And something about her appealed in a big way. He would like to take her for a long trip to Hawaii, where they could lie on beaches and talk about life and not discuss all the rest of the shit, but she also had a partner, and that was something that Corbin could not forget.

It felt damn wrong too.

He hated that he was getting possessive about a woman who wasn't single. That would never be a good deal for him. But, at the moment, all he could think about was getting her free from this current asshole.

She'd been through enough. Seeing her up front in the kidnapper's vehicle, realizing the guy was taking her someplace, Corbin wanted to just bide his time. Yet, at the same time, he couldn't let this guy get too far ahead. He quickly called Hatch while he drove. "They're right in front of me."

"Okay, now calm down."

"Yeah, already did. Anybody get to Aiden?"

"Paramedics got there a few minutes ago to check on the kids. Another team is working on Jewel."

"Good. What about this asshole I have now?"

"It'd be nice if you'd let him lead us to wherever he's trying to take Nellie."

"I imagine that will be a safe house of some kind."

"That's not a bad thing," he murmured.

"Or I crash the vehicle right here and now. I grab her and pop him one."

"Well, you could, but what if something happens to Nellie's child?"

Corbin groaned.

"And have you seen Jewel's daughter? Is there a car seat in the vehicle?"

"No, not that I can see."

"And that's another reason not to crash that vehicle. You don't know that Jewel's daughter is not in the trunk or on the floor or asleep in the back seat or whatever."

"I know that. I know that." And Corbin pounded the steering wheel in frustration.

"Stay in control."

"When have you ever known me not to be in control?"

"Well, this one seems to be pushing your buttons."

"I hate assholes like this, and you know that."

"I know."

"How is Aiden?"

"He's fine. He's also pissed off about the kids, but he's not leaving until they're taken care of."

"Yep, that's good. That's exactly where he needs to be."

"Well, according to him, he needs to be on your ass to make sure you don't do something stupid."

"I wasn't planning on doing something stupid," Corbin said in a hard voice. "But I am planning on getting her away from this asshole."

"That may be," Hatch noted, "but we still have one missing child, and, according to what intel we are getting, a couple brokers are involved. Or at least there should be two brokers involved. We're not getting very much else, so we need your guy alive."

"I talked to Frankie, the guard, before he died," Corbin stated. "An exchange was to happen tonight."

"Right, so we have to find out if anything is left at that import-export warehouse."

"Didn't you get an address?"

"I did. We've got a team on it right now, but I haven't had an update yet." He paused, then said, "Hang on. I've got them coming in now." And, with that, he logged off, only to call Corbin a few minutes later. "No sign of anyone. They're checking cameras on the closest intersections to try to run them down."

Not taking a chance of being seen by Nellie's newest kidnapper, Corbin quickly turned a corner. And then he caught back up with them a block down the road. If nothing else, it should confuse that asshole with Nellie. Corbin was all about that. Anything that would cause a distraction was good. Hatch was right. Corbin didn't dare crash the vehicle.

He wanted to reach out and just pound this guy into the ground, but they had other priorities right now, and getting Nellie safely away from him was just one of them. And Corbin didn't want to be the one who talked to Nellie's father when he found out she'd been taken *again*.

It pissed him right off to know that. Also, unfortunately, the guard he had set up to watch over Nellie and Jewel tonight wouldn't make it either. And that was something that he would have to come to terms with too.

When the vehicle turned into the parking lot of a motel. Corbin pulled around the block and came back to see it now appeared to be parked. "Would he take her to a hotel for the night? That's hardly a safe place."

He pulled into the back of a lot, hopped out, and casually walked up to the truck. But as he walked past the main door of the reception area, he saw the kidnapper getting keys to a room.

Nellie stood beside him, calm and sedate. She hugged her belly, and Corbin realized that she really was okay. And, with that, he took a deep breath and relaxed even more. This guy was giving Corbin a perfect opportunity to collect her.

As Corbin watched, the kidnapper took Nellie outside to their motel room door, got her inside. But he stayed outside, did something to the door, and then raced down to his vehicle, hopped in, and took off.

Swearing, as he ran up to her hotel room, Corbin called Hatch. "He's taken off, but he's left her in the hotel room. I've got to get her." He turned to see her face peering out the window.

He immediately kicked open the door and opened his arms. She threw herself into his arms, crying out, "We've got to go. We've got to go."

"Why? Where's he going?"

"He's going back to get the kids."

"Well, that's good. Let him."

"Why?" She stared up at him, horrified.

"Because we've already got the kids."

"Jewel's daughter?"

"No, that exchange already took place."

She stared at him fearfully. "Oh my, that poor little girl. Poor Jewel."

"I know. I know. We're looking for them. We're searching for any vehicles that were in the area."

"This guy said they were Asian. The brokers were Asian, and he's kind of scared."

"He should be."

"He killed his buddy because he thought he let us out."

"Did you tell him that's what happened?"

"No, I made him believe that he killed his buddy unnecessarily."

"Did it bother him?"

"No, I think he was just looking for an excuse that he didn't have to pay him, but, at the same time, he's kind of out of his depth, and he's sinking quickly."

"Yeah, he's devolving. I need to call Hatch and update him."

"Or we could track him down."

"We could, but your father is already in a major panic. I'll take you to the hospital and drop you off to stay with Jewel."

"No," she argued. "I think, once he finds out that the kids are gone, he'll go after the brokers."

"Why?" He stopped at the stairs and looked at her.

"Because he hasn't been paid yet."

"That was Frankie's deal too. He hadn't been paid, and neither had the kid on the ground."

"So this guy, he'll try to run, and, in order to run, he needs the money from the broker. He called me—my baby—his big payday. We have to follow him."

Corbin made a sudden decision and said, "Let's go." He raced out to his truck.

"I knew it was you," she cried out. "This was the truck that followed us."

"Yeah, I wanted to cause an accident and get you out of there, but I was afraid of hurting the baby."

She nodded. "Believe me. I thought about causing an accident too, but I just didn't want to take the chance." She looked over at him and smiled. "Thank you."

"Now we have to find him."

"Well, I can tell you that he's gone back to the warehouse."

"Or he's gone to meet the brokers."

"They need the other kids too though."

Corbin phoned Hatch. "I need a location and a direction for that truck."

"There's also been a newsbreak. Somehow it got leaked to the press that the kids at a warehouse were found by the cops."

"Shit, if this other guy heard that …"

"Yep, then he's on the run. But he still needs money. So the brokers are next."

"I need Nellie taken to a hospital, where her father can find her," Corbin said.

At that, his phone was snatched from his hand. "Like hell," Nellie snapped. "We're going after this asshole, and we need to find that little girl of Jewel's. I don't know if Jewel is still alive or not, but no way in hell that little girl will go off with whatever assholes have bought her."

"I get it," Hatch replied calmly. "We already have the other kids. And we're looking for Jewel's daughter."

"Find the brokers and find whoever bought her," she

said in a hard tone. "With everything else you guys pull off, that should be a piece of cake."

Hatch snorted. "Yeah, while we're on it, put Corbin back on."

"Only if you promise to get that little girl."

"We're doing our best. Now back to Corbin."

She handed his phone back to him and slumped in the corner of her seat.

"She's a firecracker." Hatch chuckled. "Sounds perfect for you."

"Don't even go there," he muttered, looking over at her, hoping she hadn't heard, but she was staring at him in surprise. With that, he quickly hung up.

"What was that crack about perfect for you?"

He shrugged, embarrassed. "Nothing." He gave a half laugh. "Just several of the guys on our teams have ended up finding partners in the craziness of our jobs, so they thought maybe I would find one too."

"Wow, you're not married?"

He frowned. "No. Why would I be married?"

"I don't know. I figured all the good men were."

"Well, I'll take that as a good sign"—he laughed—"but no. Besides, you already have a partner."

She stared at him. "I don't know what Kool-Aid you're sipping from, but I do *not* have a partner."

He stared at her. "You're pregnant."

She snickered. "True, and sorry, I tend to forget about that."

"How can you forget about it?" He motioned at her belly, protruding in front of her.

She smiled. "When it comes to relationships, I forget how unusual and messy it gets for me."

"Do you want to explain that?"

"Yeah, artificial insemination."

He stared at her, wide-eyed, as he drove down the highway at top speed. He heard his phone beep. "Take that, will you? It should be an address. Punch it into the GPS, please." Once that was done, Corbin asked her, "Why? Why go the artificial insemination route?"

"Because I couldn't find a decent guy, and I kept failing at relationships, so I figured, why not just skip that phase?"

"I'm not sure what you're calling decent, but we're not all assholes."

"No, not all of you apparently," she murmured, "but lots of you are."

He nodded. "I won't argue with that, but an awful lot of bitches are out there too."

"Isn't that the truth. Anyway," she muttered, "I decided that I would have a child regardless. I'm thirty so my biological clock was ticking."

"How do you feel about it now?" he muttered.

"I feel good. Yet also like I could have waited a little longer," she admitted.

He looked at her curiously, and she added, "As long as nobody else gets their hands on my child," she said fiercely, "I am good."

He looked over at her, smiled. "Nobody will."

After a moment, she asked, "I guess that makes me somebody you don't want anything to do with, *huh?*"

He frowned. "What are you talking about?"

"I'm pregnant with another man's child."

"Even if you were, that doesn't mean I wouldn't be interested in you." He grinned. "Obviously it's not my child, and you know that could have been fun getting you there."

She burst out laughing. "Well, I never had a problem with the fun part. It was always the weight of the days after that, when there just didn't seem to be anything else in the relationship."

"Ah." He nodded. "You know that an awful lot of relationships are based on sex."

"Well, I don't want one like that. Not only about the sex. I want one where I know I can wake up in the morning and see a good man beside me every day and not just on good days. Maybe that's asking for too much. I don't know."

"I don't think so. This kind of sounds similar to what I want, which is to wake up the next morning to have the same woman and to know that she's there because she wants to be there, because that's what her heart wants," he murmured quietly.

She looked over at him in delight. "Exactly."

"Yet you went ahead without me." He pointed at her belly, with a grin on his face.

She smiled. "I did, didn't I? Still, I don't regret it. Once this child became real to me, I can't regret anything about his or her existence. It's too precious."

"How can you regret it?" He looked at her in astonishment. "You're carrying another human being. I mean, somebody who's special and is counting on us to look after it right now, while it's in danger. You can't ever regret something like that," he murmured by her side. She stared at him, but he shrugged. "I was an only child. My mom tried very hard to get pregnant a second time for a long time and then finally gave it up. As it was, they were both killed in a car accident and left me alone all too soon. Yet I was old enough not to be a ward of the state and immediately signed up for the navy. That kind of changes how you view the world and how precious it is, especially to have family around."

"I'm sorry."

"How did your father feel about Baby?"

"He's beyond angry, and he wants to know who the father is, and I haven't told him."

He smiled. "Are you hiding that from him?"

"I was, which is childish of me, but, at the time, I didn't have the backbone needed. Somewhere along this lovely adventure, I've grown an awful lot of backbone."

"Trauma and strife will do that," he murmured. "Besides, it's for Baby, so it's all good."

"You haven't met my father."

"No, and I'm trying to avoid him on the phone too. When we lost you *again*? Believe me. More than a few heads rolled."

"Yeah, that sounds like him."

"On the other hand," Corbin added, looking over at her closely, "he's seriously worried. So I know he really cares."

"I know, and I need to call and to make peace with him. If nothing else, he'll be a grandfather."

"That's often enough to change everything. Most people can't wait to become a grandparent."

"Well, he just wanted me to become a wife first."

"His loss." Corbin smiled. "You needed to do something for you, and you stepped out and did it, fully prepared to accept the responsibility. If nothing else, he should be proud of that."

"I don't know about that, but thanks, I think."

"You're welcome. I respected everything I've seen about you so far," he murmured. "There's been nothing easy about these crazy last two days."

"A couple days for you seemed much longer for me."

"Exactly, and you're still holding up. It's Jewel and her daughter that you're concerned about. Absolutely no need for you to be doing anything other than what you're doing."

"I have to make sure that Jewel's daughter is okay," she said fiercely. "Jewel already had a pretty shitty life. I don't even know if she's alive or dead."

"She's in surgery."

Nellie stared at him and whispered, "Dear God."

"I know," he said quietly. "Let's hope she makes it."

"What if she doesn't?"

"I don't know what to say, but, if so, there's a good chance that her daughter will end up in foster care."

"Oh, my God, then isn't it better to let her have a family where she's loved?"

"But do you want a family where they murdered the mother to get the child?"

"No." She stared out the windshield. "And Jewel's daughter is not ending up in foster care either."

"Yeah, what will you do about it?" he asked curiously.

She smiled. "I'll adopt her as mine," she murmured. "Jewel went through hell with me. She did everything she could to save her daughter and to survive. Her daughter deserves that much."

"Ah. See? That's what I mean. I can respect that too."

"You don't think I'm crazy?"

"Hell no, and you have to do what you think is right."

"Yeah, well, you know my father won't agree."

"It doesn't matter about your father, does it? You have to do what you think is right for you."

And, with that, she settled back and closed her eyes, smiling.

CHAPTER 10

N ELLIE BOLTED UPRIGHT as the vehicle took a hard left turn. She grabbed a hold of the dash and looked over at him.

"Change of location," he said, his voice tight. "Your kidnapper is heading in a different direction."

"Do we know why?" she whispered, brushing the hair off her face. Apparently she'd dozed off. She couldn't even imagine, before getting pregnant, just how tired she would constantly be.

He shook his head. "We're still getting details."

"The fact that you're even getting details is something."

He smiled. "It is, indeed. It's just not enough."

"It's never enough." she murmured. "Is it?"

"Sometimes, yes. Sometimes all of this just plays out beautifully, ... but too often there are problems."

She hung on to her seat belt and shifted into her seat slightly, so she was a little better prepared for the rough corners. But she still didn't regret coming. She would prefer to be home, curled up in her own bed, with this whole nightmare over, all this as a distant dream. She knew everything was supposed to look better when she got a little bit of time and distance to it, and she needed that rather desperately at the moment. Just thinking of Jewel in surgery was enough to make Nellie sick to her stomach.

She looked over at Corbin, as he took another hard turn. Something was so familiar and yet not so familiar about him, and she couldn't quite shake it out of her mind.

He took another hard angle, and now they were heading back the other way that they had come.

"I hope this intel is good," she whispered.

He nodded. "Me too."

She realized that, of course, he trusted the people who were behind him too. She sank back into her seat. "God, I hope this is over soon," she whispered under her breath.

"I heard that. I still think I should have taken you back to the hospital."

"And I wouldn't go, so this is on me."

"I don't care if it's on you or not. I don't want this to be something that you come to regret. Or me."

And she knew what he meant. Her hands instinctively held her belly, as she gently massaged it and murmured to the child within, telling her or him that everything would be okay. She was kind of hoping for a little girl, but was okay with either. She'd heard stories about women seemingly knowing exactly what they were having and others having no clue. She'd be in the no-clue category. But then she'd only ever had this one pregnancy, so maybe she'd get more intuitive as time went on.

Corbin took another hard turn, and suddenly, up ahead, she saw the vehicle of the kidnapper. She leaned forward. "That's him," she gasped.

He nodded. "Yeah, and the thing is, ... he's moving really slow. He's looking for an address."

"But why?"

"Probably a new location. A new meeting place, based on the fact that the other kids have been picked up, and the brokers probably had to change everything."

"Does he really think he'll get paid?"

"Well, he thinks so. Now that he's lost the other kids, he may be hoping that the brokers haven't heard that yet. And, of course, he also has to realize that, although he took shots at his buddy, he probably doesn't know if he's dead or not."

She looked over at him. "But he is, isn't he?"

He nodded. "Yes, he definitely is."

"I'm almost sorry about that."

"Yeah, I hear you. That's a prime example of wrong-crowd, wrong-business, and a one-way street into trouble."

She winced. "Not what any of us want."

"He did tell me that he had no family to be ashamed of him and that he was grateful for that."

"How sad to think that we're grateful to die with shame on our head if nobody knows about it."

"I think, in his case, it's more that he's ashamed of what and where he went in life. He did say something also about needing to, ... you know, pay the price when he died. I've seen so much death, anguish, and pain that it's all about doing the best that you can because, before you know it, something happens without any warning, and it's over."

"That sounded like you're quoting somebody."

"A friend of mine told me that." His laughter fell away, and he pointed. "Look."

And she watched, the vehicle that they were following slowed, then slipped into a big warehouse. "Similar to where we were but still different. If it worked once, it should work twice, right?"

"I guess." Corbin stared at the vehicle.

"I still don't have a good feeling about it."

"No, neither do I. At least I don't get a good feeling for

him."

She nodded. "I guess that's what I meant. I don't want you going in there either."

"That's nice of you, but we have to find out who's got the little girl."

"And how will you do that?"

"Somebody in there is lying in wait for this guy." At that, his phone buzzed, and, as he answered it, Aiden was asking for Corbin's coordinates. Corbin quickly gave him the address where they were. "Backup is needed. Kidnapper has gone for a meeting. and I don't think he'll meet what he's expecting."

She didn't hear Aiden's answer, but it wasn't hard to decipher it. When Corbin hung up, she looked at him. "Of course you won't wait until Aiden gets here."

He shook his head. "Waiting won't get us the answers we need." He pulled off to the side. "Now I know you won't like this ..."

She groaned. "I'm supposed to wait in the vehicle."

"Not only will you wait in my truck," he said, "but you'll lie down in the back seat, and you'll not lift your head. I can't have anybody knowing you're here." Before she could say anything, he added, "That is nonnegotiable."

She stared at him for a long moment. "I hadn't even considered that."

"I know, but it is major. If anybody finds out you're here, ... you are the payoff still. Remember that both sides want you."

At that, she gripped her belly even tighter and nodded. "I'm not going anywhere." He hesitated, but she assured him, "Go. You need to find Jewel's little girl."

"Well, I don't expect the child to be here, but, chances

are, it'll be our best shot at finding the people who have taken her."

She nodded. "Go, go, go, go."

And, with that, he was gone.

She scrambled into the back seat, laid down there, found a blanket, and she pulled it over her and huddled quietly in the darkness. All she could think about was Corbin, and, at the same time, there was that odd recognition of something.

It was frustrating because she was pretty damn sure she'd seen him before. This scenario was all too familiar, but she couldn't place it. She closed her eyes and whispered to the baby, "It's okay, sweetheart. We'll get out of this. It's okay."

Now in the darkness all alone, she realized just how foolish it was that she'd come. She had no phone to call for help; she had no backup, and she had no way to defend herself. And that had been all on her, which was absolutely zero help right now, when she was alone in the dark. Surely Corbin would get back soon.

She also knew she was asking for a bloody miracle. She thought about the other times in her life when she'd asked for miracles and realized there was absolutely no reason not to ask for another one. She closed her eyes and whispered a prayer to the world around her.

"Please let us get out of this safe. I know I got a rescue. I know that, in many ways, some people would say I blew it, but it's not what it looks like. I'm honestly trying to help another little girl because her mom is in surgery, and I know, when Jewel wakes up, she'll desperately want to know where her girl is. We're doing what we can for her. Please, another miracle would be lovely."

And, with that, she closed her eyes and endured the long cold wait.

As soon Corbin was out of the vehicle and heading toward the warehouse in question, he sent a message to Hatch, asking for security and backup for Nellie. He hated to leave her alone. He was taking a risk, and it didn't sit well. If anything happened to her ...

Hatch sent a text. **I sent two units to your location. They are en route. ETA seven minutes.**

And, with that, Corbin had to trust that somebody would come and stand guard. He would have preferred Aiden, but Corbin needed his partner's help inside. With that, he flattened himself up against the building. Down at the far end, he saw a halo of light.

He crept his way closer, listening carefully, but the silence of the night was absolute. Obviously this location was picked for a reason. Still any sound, any noise would cause a shot to be fired, which would ring out in this darkness in a horrific way.

Maybe they didn't care. Maybe nobody was around. And maybe they wouldn't even bother with a gun. He had no way to know what these other two people, the brokers, were like, and if they were even here. For all Corbin knew, a hired gun had been brought in to make this all go away. Corbin had seen other things along that line, time and time again. Hearing something faint, he headed toward it.

As he got closer, he thought he heard a voice.

"No, I need to get paid now." That voice held a note of desperation.

Several voices spoke at the same time, and Corbin realized that either they weren't prepared to shoot him right now, or they were looking for information from him.

They were probably trying to figure out where he'd stashed Nellie. She was worth a lot of money in this equation.

He crept forward in the darkness and found a window covered in dirt, showing the years of neglect this decrepit building had seen. He cleaned a spot to see inside.

And saw the asshole they'd been following. But the person he was talking to was just out of Corbin's line of sight. He shifted, so he could look from another angle. The man sat at a table, his back to Corbin.

"I have to have the money."

"And we have to have the girl."

"And that's fine," he murmured. "You can have the girl. I thought you wanted me to keep her until she was due."

"No, we'll take care of that."

The kidnapper frowned and then shrugged. "Fine, that's probably a better idea anyway."

"Why is that?" one man asked, looking at him.

"Pregnant women kind of give me the heebie-jeebies."

The other man started. "And yet you were totally okay to go with it before."

"Sure, I mean, how much trouble can they be? They're the size of a beach turtle. At least this one is very docile."

"And that's a good thing," the same man said in a snide voice.

"Now what about my payment?"

"I told you, until we get paid for the little girl, we can't pay you."

"I can't believe you let anybody take that little girl without payment in the first place," he snapped.

"And sometimes things have to happen in their own time frame. We know this couple, so we have no problem letting them have the child ahead of time, and the child needed care so …"

"She was fine though."

"Sure, she was fine, but she was also struggling without her mother. She needed the fastest adjustment possible."

Corbin wasn't so sure if that was just a cop-out or if the child really needed *adjustment* time. However, if she'd missed her mother, or had thought something was wrong, or she'd been hurt in any way, then it would make sense.

"That's fine, but I've also got to pay Frankie."

The guy looked at him. "I highly doubt you'll pay Frankie, particularly if you won't be looking after the pregnant women anymore."

"Frankie still needs something for his time. I'll never get him to help me on another job if I don't pay him."

"Okay, that makes sense," the guy said. "I'll check to see what I have available right now." And, with that, it looked like he was opening a laptop.

"Just write me a check." The kidnapper looked around nervously.

The guy shook his head. "If you give me a chance to check how much money is available, I could probably write you a decent check."

"Where's your partner? I don't have time to wait."

"What's the rush?"

He threw up his hands. "I don't like the fact that I haven't been paid. I won't do a job like this again without payment upfront."

"No, neither will we," he agreed quietly, "but it is what it is this time around. So we're all making the best of it."

"But that's your decision. I was supposed to get payment as soon as I gave you the child. Now you want me to give you the woman too, without payment."

"Are you telling me that you won't give us the woman?" he asked, raising his head and staring down the kidnapper.

"No, I'm not saying that," he immediately backtracked. "I'm trying to say that I need to get paid."

"I'm checking the accounts to see what we have available."

The kidnapper looked beyond frustrated. And, of course, for the broker, it was a stalling tactic, but what for? Corbin waited and watched, wondering where the second broker was. When a door opened on the other side of the room, Corbin smiled, as the second broker walked in.

"Hey," the first broker said, "he needs some money now."

"Of course he does," the second broker responded in a silky voice that sent shivers down Corbin's spine.

"I need payment," the kidnapper repeated in a tone above a grovel. "I let you do the other one on credit, but I can't do that now. I've got to pay for her at the hotel."

"Which hotel?" the seated broker asked. "We can cover that immediately."

"That's not the answer." The kidnapper shook his head. "If I give you the hotel, ... you won't have any reason to pay me at all."

The second broker stared at the kidnapper in shock. "Hey, we've been working together for quite a while. Let's not mess that up now."

The kidnapper seemed to relax slightly. "Yeah, I know, but I need payment. This is why I do this job."

"No, I get that." The seated guy looked over at his buddy. "We can give him half."

The other broker shrugged. "Sure, we can give him half.

It'll leave us tight."

At that, Nellie's captor seemed to relax a little further yet again. "So just write me a check right now for half. I'll come back with the girl and get the rest."

"And when will you deliver her?" the first broker asked warily. "Because we need the woman. Remember that you won't be looking after her anymore."

"Yeah, right. You can give me the other half when I deliver her. Tomorrow."

"No, I need her tonight."

"Tonight?" He repeated. "What's the rush?"

"We want to get her out of here and into a medical facility, where we can keep a better eye on her. If you know any other pregnant woman in a good position for this, let us know."

"Sure."

The seated broker wrote him a check and handed it to him. "There you go. Now where are we picking up the woman?"

The kidnapper hesitated, then he named the hotel.

"Good. What room? I'll send someone for her. Does she need an ambulance?" he asked from his laptop, looking up.

"No, she's fine. She's ambulatory, just scared."

"And you left her alone in the room?"

"Sure, but I also set the door, so she can't open it."

"From the inside, I presume."

"Yeah, of course. Obviously I won't lose the asset."

"Good. What about other pregnant women?"

"No, I don't know of any. Which is frustrating, considering how much money this one's worth."

"Right, all we need to do is find some more. Preferably further along, so we don't have this long wait."

"What about women who go to sperm banks?"

The second broker nodded. "That's another option too," he said thoughtfully. "Good call. Will you head back to the hotel now?"

"I have to get this check cashed."

"If you go to a loan shark, you'll lose most of it."

"I know, but I don't have any choice. I need money." And, with that, he made a dash for the door. As his hand reached for the knob, a single gunshot rang out. He stopped at the door and slowly collapsed against it, before sliding to the floor.

CHAPTER 11

NELLIE WOKE WITH a start, only to see nothing but darkness around her. Yet she heard voices. Two people talking. She wasn't even sure who it was or what they were saying, but then she recognized one of them. She sat upright to see Aiden, standing beside Corbin's vehicle. He bent and nodded. "Hey, glad you're okay."

"Where's Corbin?" she whispered.

"He's inside."

She stared at him. "You need to go help him."

"I'm on the way, and we have security here for you too.'

She looked at the man and frowned; he just stared right back at her. She shrugged, and opened the door slightly so she could speak with Aiden. "If you say it's safe, but I'm more concerned about Corbin."

"I'm heading in now. I heard a shot a few minutes ago." And, with that, he disappeared.

She looked over at the stranger and smiled at him tentatively. "Thank you."

He shrugged. "I'm an off-duty cop right now, but obviously something pretty ugly is going down here."

She nodded. "Remember those kidnapped kids who were found in a warehouse?" He looked at her and nodded. "One of the kidnappers is in there. Along with the brokers for the children."

His expression darkened, and he turned to face the warehouse. "Well, that's shitty. I'd rather be in there myself."

"I was one of the kidnap victims. They're after my baby." And she patted her rather round stomach.

"Jesus." He opened the front door and just sat down in the front seat.

"Maybe we should get out now. I am not at all sure about sitting here."

"You mean, more than likely, you have to go to the bathroom," he said, with a note of humor.

She looked at him in surprise.

"I've got three kids. After you've lived with a pregnant woman for a little bit, you understand that every bathroom is mapped out for you on all your local routes." He laughed. "Generally by the time the nine months are done, you have hit them all every time you go out."

The wry tone to his voice was so genuine that she had to laugh. "Right," she admitted, "I really could use a bathroom."

"The only thing I can offer you is the other side of the vehicle."

She winced. "I won't have much choice." She struggled to get out of the vehicle and made her way over to another one, a big delivery van, parked alongside Corbin's truck. She squatted behind to relieve herself, hating that she was in this state. She pulled a Kleenex from her pocket that she had stuffed there from the hotel. By the time she came back around, her guard sat there, looking at her, a grin on his face. "Feeling better?"

"Much. Whoever thought pregnancy was a good idea is an idiot."

He laughed. "Well, I'm sure, design-wise, it could use a

little bit of an adjustment, especially from your viewpoint."

She nodded. "Yeah, more than a little bit. I can't imagine that this was literally the best design that anybody could think of."

"Hey, it works, so it's all good."

She wasn't so sure about the *all good* part. But he seemed to be quite content with it. She sat back down in the vehicle, groaning slightly.

He looked over at her. "Are you okay?"

She nodded. "Just getting nervous that they've been gone so long."

He nodded. "We need to trust that they know what they're doing."

"Yeah, well, I'd feel better if there was a hell of a lot more people involved," she murmured.

"Well, I'm not leaving you. They'd have my head if anything happened to you."

She smiled at that. "He's already rescued me twice."

At that, the cop stared at her. "Twice?"

She nodded. "Yeah, so I'm not going anywhere, and I appreciate that you're staying here with me."

"I'm here," he said, "but I sure wish I knew what they were doing in there."

And that was a sentiment that she agreed with completely.

CORBIN WATCHED THE two brokers gather up their stuff, talking quietly together. Obviously they were completely unconcerned about the body on the ground.

Corbin found that interesting because it took a pretty

hardened person to completely accept killing a man, letting him bleed out on the floor. Considering that this warehouse could be part of their own export organization, they were not concerned at all.

Just then one of their phones rang, and the broker switched to English. "No, I ran into a problem. I need you to take care of it." He turned to look at the body. "How much?" he asked, then listened for the reply. "What do you mean? Why is it so much more?" he snapped, getting visibly angry. At that, he stared at his partner. "I'll call you back." He turned to his partner. "So apparently he heard about the kids being collected on the news."

"Of course he did." The second broker turned to stare at the dead man in disgust. "We need the pregnant woman picked up and now."

"I'm wondering if we should do the job ourselves," his partner said in a low tone.

The other man nodded. "We can do that."

"What about the little girl?"

"What about her? She's already been taken possession of."

"I know. I just wonder if there's anything that can lead them to us?"

"This laptop, our cell phones, the usual."

He nodded again. "Do you think we should warn the parents, tell them to get out of the country?"

"They knew the risks, before they ever got into this. It's not our fault they saw the little girl in town and heard the mom yelling at her and figured they could give her a better life. This is definitely a case where we need to butt out. If they get caught, that's up to them."

His partner nodded. "In that case, let's pick up that

pregnant woman and get the hell out of here fast."

"How hot do you think things are getting?"

"We're not prepared to lose the pregnant woman. That's a given."

"No, and I'm not suggesting that." He pushed his hair off his face. "But, depending on what this asshole has done, we might find ourselves in a bigger pickle than we expected."

"That'll never go down well."

"No. Right now let's get the woman from the hotel, and then we'll make plans."

"I'd rather make plans and then get the woman."

"We have a few hours at least, until this building wakes up. And that guy will never wake up, so we need to get rid of him and then get her. But the longer we leave her unattended, the more chances we have of losing her." He stared at his partner. "What are the chances she's even at that hotel?" He looked down at the dead man. "What are the chances he lied to us?"

"I hate to say it, but it's possible. We need to check."

That completely caught the first broker by surprise.

The second broker walked to the door. "I'll go check. You stay here and see if you can arrange to get this body taken care of. I'll call you as soon as I have her."

And, with that, not even giving his partner a chance to say something, he raced out.

That was odd. Something about that just didn't sit well with Corbin. Just as he was about to step in and confront the first broker, the second broker returned. He was carrying a man. *Nellie's guard.* Corbin's blood ran cold when he realized just what had happened. *Where the hell is Aiden?*

At that, Aiden appeared beside him. "Who shot who?"

Corbin stared at Aiden in horror, as he pointed. "That's

the guard you left with her?"

"This has gone on long enough," the second broker roared, as he dropped the guard to the ground. "We've had so many fuckups."

"We need to get the woman."

"Yeah, well, the pregnant woman is outside," he snapped.

His partner stared at him. "What do you mean, she's outside?"

"She's sitting in a vehicle outside. I just knocked her out," he snapped. "This guy was keeping an eye on her. Now we have to get rid of this one too. Did you find anybody to deal with this?"

He shook his head. "No. Right now, everybody's saying it's too hot to touch."

"Somebody's always saying that bullshit. We have to get the hell out of here. We'll just torch the place." And, with that, he turned, grabbed gasoline cans off to the side, and poured it all around.

"Well hell," the first broker cried out. "I wouldn't be at all surprised if our asshole here didn't set that up too."

"He won't be around anymore to give us any trouble, so that's not a problem."

"He's not a problem, but, dammit, this operation is becoming quite a headache."

The second broker looked at the first. "So what do you want to do?"

"You know what I want to do." He sighed, looked at his partner, and said, "You know it's been a good run, but this is definitely not a good business model."

The second guy didn't even give the first guy a chance to say more before he fired a single gunshot, and his partner went down, with a bullet exiting the back of his head.

"Well, *that's* what I want to do," he snapped at the dead man. "I should have done that a fucking long time ago." He stared around and said, "You know something? ... I should just kill her too. I can't handle her alone, and I don't want any of this headache." With that, he disappeared immediately.

Aiden raced out into the darkness, back to Corbin's truck.

Corbin quickly—and as silently as he could—broke the window he had been staring through. Before he could climb inside, the gunman returned, hauling an unconscious Nellie over his shoulder. He laid her down. "I don't really give a shit how many bodies they find, as long as there's nothing to pin me to it." He turned immediately, grabbed the laptop, stole his partner's cell phone and wallet and keys. Thereafter he lit a match and set the place on fire and bolted.

Corbin had to trust that Aiden would get the partner. But Corbin had one thing and one thing only on his mind, and that was rescuing whomever was left alive in that building, particularly one person. He jumped in through the window, choking at the smoke already taking over the building. The structure was dry, old, and catching fire fast. He bolted inside, but it took him longer than he expected to get to Nellie.

The sounds of the crackling building got stronger and stronger all around him. He headed for the guard and for Nellie. Checking for a pulse, he realized they were both alive. And that would compound his problem.

There was absolutely no winning here. He had to get them both out; any other answer was unacceptable. He picked up the guard, threw him over a shoulder, bent down, carrying his weight on his back, then pulled Nellie into his arms, still bent over her in a huddle, with her crouched in his arms, as he slowly made his way to the door. The smoke was thick, and oxygen was scarce. His heart slammed against his chest, as he gave a hearty back kick to the door. Of course it was locked. It took several kicks, but desperation had fueled him.

Outside, coughing, he stumbled, as he moved far enough away that he placed both of them on the ground. Nellie started coughing almost immediately.

"It's okay," he said. "Just take a moment and breathe."

She stared up at him. "Dear God," she cried out. "Now I know why you look familiar."

He didn't have time to talk to her, having started CPR on the guard, until the guard started to choke and gasp in front of him. Then he picked up the guard and moved him a good one hundred yards away. Nellie slowly followed. Clear of the cackling fire and smoke from the burning building, he just held her close.

"God, that was rough," she whispered, from the safety of his arms.

"Too rough."

She stared at him. "Did you get everybody?"

"I got everybody who was alive. It's another case of no honor among thieves."

She stared at him, not comprehending.

"One of the two brokers shot your kidnapper, then apparently knocked out your guard and you. Then he decided that enough was enough, and he shot his own partner, then dragged you and your guard inside, where he lit the building on fire."

"Good God." She stared at him in shock and turned to

look at the building. And almost immediately started to cough again.

He stayed at her side, until a rescue unit showed up. Then he let the paramedics take over. As she was being loaded up, she looked over at him. "Are you coming?"

"I'll meet you at the hospital."

"You're not getting away that fast." She reached out a hand.

He walked over to grasp hers. "Getting away from what?"

She smiled. "The whole time that I was captive, after I saw the photo of you, I knew you looked familiar, but I couldn't place you." He shrugged. She shook her head. "Oh no you don't. I don't really understood why, but I put it down to the stress of the occasion." She laughed, then coughed. When she could speak again, she added, "But now I finally realize who you are."

"And who am I?" he asked warily.

She smiled. "You're the one who rescued me from that fire two decades ago. Only you were just a kid then."

He stared at her and slowly nodded. "I didn't think you remembered."

"I didn't initially," she whispered, regret in her voice, and then started to cough again.

"Stop trying to talk."

She gave him a good frown back. "I'll talk when I want to talk," she snapped. "but don't think you're disappearing from my life again."

"Hey, you disappeared from my life a long time ago," he replied in a wry tone.

"No, that was my dad. Believe me. I had a major fight about it then."

He stared at her, but she was quickly loaded up and taken away. He turned to see Aiden, standing here, his arms full of electronics. "Hey."

"How are you?" Aiden asked.

"I'm fine." Corbin smiled. "At least I got them out."

He nodded. "And I got the asshole and all the electronics. Now let's put our heads together and see if we can find where that little girl is."

"How about we find an all-night coffee shop? I really could use something for my throat."

At that, Aiden stopped, stared at him, "Do you need to get checked out?"

Corbin gave Aiden a hard look. "We won't even discuss that."

His partner laughed. "Still the hard-ass."

"Always."

As they walked to the truck, Aiden said, "I also heard something in that conversation. Did you rescue her many years ago?"

Corbin gave a bark of laughter. "Apparently, yes. It showed up when Hatch sent me her file. I just couldn't believe it. Of course she didn't recognize me, but it was a long time ago."

"How long ago?"

"Twenty years." He smiled. "Twenty long years."

"Don't tell me that you've been holding that torch for decades?"

"No, not at all." He laughed. "I knew I'd probably never see her again. I lived in the same apartment building where the fire happened. I knew the people who lived there and ended up bringing Nellie and her friend's mother to my place, to the patio, where we were rescued."

"What happened?"

"She was having a sleepover at a friend's house. The building caught fire, and her girlfriend perished."

"Oh, crap. And why were you living in England back then?"

Corbin shrugged. "My parents loved to travel, and sometimes their work required it too. I'm so glad we had that time together, before they were gone. I caught the travel bug too."

Aiden shook his head. "So how old were the two of you during this long-ago fire?"

"She was ten. I had just turned eleven. But remember in one of my witness statements? Nellie had an attempted kidnapping when she was sixteen. Now all this has been repeated in the last two days. So, yeah, it also explains why her father is beyond protective."

"It sure does," Aiden agreed.

"Nothing quite like coming close to losing a child. In this case the only child he has," Corbin added.

"But she is now safe and sound," Aiden reminded him.

"Thank God for that. If I have to rescue that girl one more time, I'll chain her to me, so she can't get into any more trouble."

At that, Aiden laughed. "You know something? I don't think she'd argue."

At a nearby coffee shop, Corbin ordered a large glass of water and a cup of coffee, while they pored over the broker's laptop that they now had. Hatch gave them an update on the condition for Nellie, her baby, and her most recent guard. Corbin nodded. "Apparently they'll all be fine," he shared with Aiden, as Corbin read the latest text from Hatch.

"Did you expect anything else?"

"No, not necessarily, except I was worried about the baby. So it's just nice to see it in writing. Nellie's also asking for me."

"Of course she is, particularly now that you have something else to talk about."

Corbin rolled his eyes at that. "I was just a dumb kid. If that had been my son rushing into a raging fire on the third floor, I'd have kicked his butt for doing something so risky."

At that, Aiden laughed. "And yet you saved a life—two lives."

"I did, and it set me on a path into the navy. I wanted more of that hero stuff."

"Obviously it was a good thing that you did go down that pathway because look. You got Nellie."

He looked over at his friend and frowned. "What are you talking about?"

"Whatever this romance thing you Mavericks have going on, obviously this one was yours. I mean, you did have a prior claim and all."

At that, he sighed. "I guess, in a way, but not really."

His friend laughed. "I'll be interested to see how her dad feels about this."

"I don't know how her dad will feel about it. Not too worried about it either way."

"But the question really is, how do you feel about *her*?"

He gave his friend a lopsided grin. "Let's just say that I don't want to let her out of my sight—in case she gets into trouble again."

"Sure. Like I believe that." And, with that, they focused on the material in front of them.

And then something in the brokers' bank records caught Corbin's gaze. "What's right here?" He tapped the laptop screen. "This payment? The broker just got paid, put it into the bank account, and then the emails. Look at that invoice."

"I really don't want to hear that information but feel like I need to. So what does a one-year-old little girl give these guys?"

"In this case, about one hundred thousand reasons to kidnap her."

At that, Aiden whistled. "That's a lot of money."

"It *is* a lot of money. The brokers said something about how the adoptive parents saw the little girl in town and didn't like the way her mom talked to her. They'd been trying to go through an adoption agency, but he had a criminal record, which meant that no way they would be approved. They decided to take things into their own hands and to get this little girl for themselves. Absolutely positive that they could give her a better life than what she was having with Jewel."

"And you know something? Jewel may not have been the perfect mother, but I bet she put a whole lot more effort into it than these bozos thought."

"I think she was also stressed out, trying to pay the bills, trying to raise a child, and trying to do all the good things that go along with that," Corbin said. "What we need now is an address."

"Have we got one?"

He nodded. "Yeah, sure looks like it." He quickly sent the information to Hatch, then called him. "This looks like an address where the little girl who was sold has been taken. Can you do a search on the owners for that property?"

Hatch came back a little bit later, and gave them the names of the adoptive couple.

"Let's go pay a visit," Corbin said. "Two women in the

hospital want to know that that little girl is safe right now."

"I hear you," Aiden replied.

Corbin stood. "Could've used some food."

"Afterward." Aiden smiled. "Afterward you'll get all kinds of accolades and food."

"Don't give a shit about the accolades. I just want to see a little girl reunited with her mother."

"You and me both," Aiden said. "So let's go be heroes once again."

CHAPTER 12

NELLIE WOKE UP slowly, getting her bearings, and stared around, panicked. She stared at the seated stranger in confusion. Then, noting the nurse's scrubs, Nellie relaxed in the hospital bed, trying to process how she got here. "What happened? I can't remember …"

The nurse immediately rushed to her side. "You're fine. You're in a hospital. That's to be expected. You've been through quite an ordeal."

"Corbin, where's Corbin?" she asked suddenly.

The nurse smiled. "Corbin's not here yet. Your father is though." She gave a half laugh. "He's not taking no for an answer on seeing you. He's been waiting for hours."

"That sounds like him." Nellie gave the nurse a wry look. "You can let him in."

"Are you sure that you're up for it?"

"He's my father. He can be an ass, but I know it's because he cares."

At that, the curtain pushed aside, and her father stepped in, glaring at her. "Well, I'm glad you finally seem to understand that much."

She glared right back at him. "Hey, Dad, if you're going to yell at me, you can leave right now because I feel like shit already."

Immediately his face softened, and he stood by her side.

"The doctor did say that you'll be fine."

"Sure." Her hand automatically went to her belly. "I'll be fine. Baby will be fine, but it was a hell of a rough few days."

"I'm so sorry you endured that. I still don't quite understand how all this came about."

"I don't know everything, so I'm not sure there's any easy answer either," she murmured. "I'm waiting for Corbin to get back. Corbin knows so much more."

At that, the nurse stepped closer to check Nellie's blood pressure.

Nellie asked her, "Do you have any update on Jewel?"

The woman looked at her with a frown. "I'm sorry. I don't know who Jewel is." And then she quickly dashed away, most likely to get away from her father. She looked at her father. "Do you have to scare everybody away?"

He snorted. "I don't suffer fools easily. You know that."

"That may be, but everybody here is just trying to do their job."

"Then they should do a better job at it," he snapped.

She glared at him. "See? This is how you chase everybody away."

He stopped and stared at her. "What do you mean?" he asked hesitantly.

"You're always so angry. Always so determined to be right and always expecting more out of everybody else around you. You make it very impossible to live with you." He frowned and stared at her. "No, that's not necessarily why I left." She waved a hand. "But it's definitely one of the reasons why I didn't stay in touch very much."

He stared down at her. "I figured it was about the baby."

"Well, the baby is a big part of it. Why should I subject

myself to your criticism and negativity when I'm already in a position that I'm so happy about? Especially when I knew you'd never accept my decision. You'll never accept that."

"I didn't say I would *never* accept it," he protested. "I would just like to see you married."

"Well, that's nice, but times have changed. I don't have to be married to have this child." He opened his mouth to protest and then snapped it shut. "Good." She smiled. "That's progress." He glared at her. "Nothing is perfect in this life," she murmured, feeling her head starting to ache. "Including you and me, and the sooner you allow all of us to be who we are, the easier it will be on you—and the people around you."

He sat down in the visitor's chair, almost stumped by her words. "So does that mean you won't tell me who the father is?" he asked hesitantly.

"Why? So you can turn around and charge him for deserting me?" she asked in a wry tone. "Why the hell would I do that?"

At that, he looked momentarily ashamed. "Is it wrong for a father to want to know that his daughter is safe?"

"Well, considering what I've just been through, I don't consider it wrong. It just seems like maybe that's not very doable." He stared at her in shock, she shrugged. "I mean, look at the last couple days."

He nodded slowly. "And I get that, and I'm even more concerned now. I also feel guilty as hell for everything that's happened to you."

"At least my baby and I are okay now, and, with any luck, this will be the end of a very ugly chapter in my life."

He nodded quietly. "You know that I just want you to be safe and happy, right?"

"You want me to be safe. I don't think the happiness factor really enters into your consideration." He stared in total confusion. She shrugged. "Come on. Look at the way you've been acting. If I was unhappy, I would have fixed it myself," she muttered, "but you weren't interested in *me* fixing anything or me being happy or unhappy. You just want me to do what you want me to do, so *you* would be happy. That is your fix for everything."

"That's not true," he protested. She gave him a hard look, and he quickly subsided. "Look. It's not that as much as I just want to make sure that you're okay. Having a baby isn't the easiest thing."

"I know. You raised me mostly on your own for a very long time, so, of course, you have firsthand experience. But I may want something different for my child and me." The problem with her father was, he was just a little too eager to express his experience at every turn as the *only* way to do things. She looked over at him. "Do you know anything about the man who rescued me?"

He shook his head. "No, I presumed he was with one of those secret service specialties, some special ops SWAT team guy."

She snorted. "Well, that's one way to look at it." She shook her head at her father's still impossible nature.

"Apparently I've said the wrong thing again."

"It's not that you've said the wrong thing"—she glowered—"it's just so very *you*."

"And you obviously didn't like that either."

She sighed. "Remember a long time ago, the fire?"

"How could I forget."

She nodded. "And because of that, you've been super ... *incredibly* overprotective of me all this time."

"Of course. I almost lost you."

"Did you ever stay in touch with the kid who saved me?"

"No." Surprised, he shook his head. "Why would I? He was just a kid."

"Sure, but he also grew up into a hell of a man." He stared at her, shaking his head, not following. "It's the same man who rescued me this time."

He reared back. "What?"

She nodded. "Somehow Corbin ended up being the one who just rescued me all over again. I didn't even recognize him, until this evening." Sagging into the hospital bed, her eyes closing voluntarily, then she started to cough. Her father was at her side instantly. She held up her hand to stop him, and then, when she could finally breathe again, she added, "It's just smoke."

"Yeah, but a lot of smoke," he said worriedly, his fear revealed that something was seriously wrong with her.

"We're fine, or rather we will be. My baby and I just need some fresh air."

"Do you want some oxygen? I can get them to bring you some oxygen."

"No, I have to just clear this crap from my lungs to protect my baby. And we'll be fine, or, at least, … we will be, when I get some good news from Corbin that Jewel is fine and that Jewel's little girl will be okay." She accepted the glass of water from her father and took a sip. When she was done, she sank back on the bed. "But, yes, it's Corbin."

He stared at her. "Did he tell you that?" he asked and frowned, as if not trusting the information.

"No, not until I finally recognized him. Something was nagging me about him from the very first time I saw his picture, and then, every time I looked at him, it nagged at me more."

"What picture?"

She quickly explained what the kidnappers had done. He shook his head at that. "That would be foolish of them, wouldn't it?"

"They weren't exactly the brainiacs in the bunch. Although I don't think any of them are alive at this point."

"Well, that's good," he snapped. "Then I don't have to waste my time prosecuting the hell out of them to ensure that they never see daylight again."

"They won't now. I think they were both shot by their supposed partners."

"Well, that's typical."

"You know what? If you want to do something for me," she murmured, "you could go find out about the condition of the other woman who was held prisoner with me." He looked at her in surprise. "Her name is Jewel. It's her daughter that Corbin is trying to track down right now."

Her dad hesitated and then got to his feet. "If it will make you feel better."

"It'll make me feel a lot better to find out she survived her surgery. I know she was gut shot, just as I was hauled out of the room."

Her father winced at that and disappeared around the curtain. She relaxed again in the bed. Getting information was something he was good at, so hopefully he could roust up some report on Jewel. And, in the meantime, Nellie wanted to hear from Corbin.

Jewel's daughter was one thing; Corbin himself was another. The man couldn't keep tempting fate like he was, as often as he did, without getting his ass kicked at one point in time. She closed her eyes for a bit. When she opened them, the nurse was taking her blood pressure again. "Did I fall asleep again?" Nellie murmured.

"You did," she said cheerfully. "It's the best thing for you."

"Is my baby okay?"

"Your baby is doing just fine," the woman reassured her.

"What about Corbin? Is he back?

The woman looked confused and then shrugged. "Your father is here. I moved him outside, so that I could take your stats."

"May I see him again?"

The nurse nodded. "As soon as I'm done." And, with that, she quickly finished her checkup, and then her father returned to the room.

He stepped up and looked down at her, worried.

"Hey, it's normal at this stage to sleep lots, after what I've been through. Plus, I was sleeping a lot before the kidnapping, just because I'm pregnant. I'm perfectly fine."

"I hope so."

"Jewel? What did you find out?"

"She's out of surgery and holding her own."

"Well, that is good news," she cried out in delight.

He nodded. "And it's her child, I guess, the men are after now, but I haven't any update on her yet."

"There were five kidnapped children. Four were rescued, but ... Jewel's daughter had already been sold."

He winced at that. "God, what a world we live in."

"It sucks, but, at the same time, people like Corbin are out there, who keep saving the day."

He looked over at her. "Sounds like you and he hit it off."

"Honestly, I think I've always had a bit of a crush on

him." She laughed. "I mean, how do you not, when the man saved my life the first time and just came back in the nick of time to do it all over again."

He frowned at that. "That doesn't sound like a woman who's having another man's baby."

"I *am* having another man's baby." Finally making a decision, she took a deep breath and said, "Sit back and relax. You won't like this."

"No, I probably won't," he bit off, "but, if it's the truth, I'd be very happy to hear it."

She smiled. "I went to a sperm bank."

His butt hit the chair, as if his legs fell out from under him. "You what? Why?"

"Because I'd had some pretty lousy relationships, and I figured that one true love would never happen for me. I'm also thirty, and my biological clock was ticking, so I decided I wouldn't wait anymore." He just stared at her, as if the concept were so foreign. "I'm an adult, Dad, and I get to make my own decisions."

He nodded slowly. "Well, you certainly made it in this case, didn't you?"

"I did, and I don't regret it one bit."

"Maybe not." He looked over at her. "But here you're talking about Corbin."

"Yeah, and I would absolutely love to spend some time with him."

"How will he feel that you're carrying another man's baby?" he pointed out.

She stared at him. "You know something? I already asked him that." Her dad stared at her in shock. She shrugged. "There's nothing quite like having life flash before your eyes—not once but twice, now three times—to make you realize that life is too short. This is something I really wanted to know, and asking him simple questions like that just happened automatically."

He let out a slow breath.

"Yeah, I'm an adult," she stated in a dry tone. "And it'd be really nice if you'd start appreciating that fact."

He nodded slowly. "When do I meet this Corbin guy?"

"How about now?" Corbin asked, as he pushed aside the curtain and stepped in. He then completely ignored her father and looked over at Nellie on the bed and grinned. "Now that's what I like to see. For once, you're safe and sound."

She opened up her arms. He walked over and gave her the gentlest of hugs. "How are you and Baby doing?"

"Now that I know you're safe, we're fine."

He smiled. "Remember? I'm the one who gets to do the rescue. I'm not the one who gets rescued."

She gave him a gentle slap on the cheek. "You can't keep tempting fate, or, at one point in time, fate will tempt back, and it'll win, not you."

"Something I have considered time and time again."

"And yet?"

"And yet what?" he asked, with an innocent look in her direction.

Her father cleared his throat. She looked over at him and smiled. "Dad, this is Corbin, the man responsible for saving my life yet again."

At that, her father looked at her, slowly standing to face Corbin. "Seriously, are you that eleven-year-old kid who rescued my daughter from the fire?"

Corbin smiled and shook the man's hand. "Yes. That rescue led me to the navy."

Her dad just looked at him in consternation. "The thought of having you on the spot to rescue her again ..."

"I was called in for the op, so it was hardly a matter of *being on the spot.*"

"Ah." Obviously her dad still was perplexed. He looked over at her.

"And that's a good thing," she reminded her dad, "because I can't imagine what it would have been like if Corbin hadn't rescued me from that place, saving my baby from those awful men."

Her father immediately reached out a hand. "But you were," he stated firmly, "so no more dwelling on it."

She snorted. "Great, Dad. Just because you order me to *stop dwelling on it* doesn't mean it'll work instantly."

"Nope," he said. "It's a process. Eventually it'll become a distant memory."

She smiled at Corbin. "That is probably the best I can hope for, isn't it?"

"You know that it's not a bad thing to hope for," Corbin murmured. "Jewel will be fairly traumatized over this entire thing as well."

Nellie winced at that. "I know." She looked up at Corbin. "Her daughter?"

He smiled. "We got the little girl. She's being checked over by the doctors right now. More so, social services will take her until Jewel is able to get back on her feet. We're combing through the sellers lives to see if there any others involved. The purchasers have also been picked up. So that thread has been taken care of too."

"That's all good news." Nellie stared at Corbin in delight. "Jewel might have family too who can help her and her daughter."

"My team is on it, but you have a responsibility to look after you and Baby. Let other people do their jobs."

"I suppose it's good that she listens to you more than she listens to me," her father snapped from beside her.

She glared at him. "Maybe because Corbin talks to me and doesn't yell at me." She turned, looking back at Corbin now. "Did you get checked out?"

"I'm fine." He gave a dismissive wave. "I am now off duty, so I came to bust you loose."

"Seriously?" she asked in delight, hardly daring to hope.

"Unless you want to stay in the hospital?"

She looked over at her father in shock, whose face was getting redder by the second, and then she threw back the blankets and cried out, "Hell, no. Get me outta here."

"Wait," her father protested. "You're not in very good shape. Don't you think you should stay overnight?"

"If my mental health has anything to do with my physical healing, then I absolutely will get better once I am out of here." She smiled at Corbin, then stood. "Dad, I'll let you know how I'm doing tomorrow morning." She walked over and gave her father a hug. "I really do love you."

His arms closed around her tightly. "We need to talk this through."

"No. You just need to accept my decisions for my life." She smiled again. "But we aren't having that discussion right now. I'll take what freedom I can get right now."

He nodded reluctantly, and she turned to look at Corbin and said, "Let's go, before anybody here changes his mind."

Corbin laughed. "Nobody will change their mind. We're free to leave, … but there is one caveat."

"What's that?" she asked.

Corbin nudged a wheelchair toward her.

She shrugged. "That's fine. It could have been so much worse, and it's still better to have you as a nursemaid than to be stuck in the hospital."

"That's what I figured," he agreed. "Besides, I need some sleep."

"Me too," she muttered, "although I do nothing but nap lately."

Her father walked out to the front door with them. "Where are you going?" he asked her.

She heard the worry in his voice. She looked back at Corbin. "Good question. Corbin, where are we going?"

"I thought your place, unless you want to go to a hotel."

"No, my place is fine."

Her dad stepped up, gave her a hug, and then a kiss on her cheek. "I'll call tomorrow to see how you are." Then he gave Corbin a curt nod and left.

She waved goodbye to her dad, then smiled, as if suddenly realizing that this horror was over, and she could live her life again. "My God, it's hard to believe I can finally go home."

"I hope it is a good thing, but it could be a little early to tell."

"No, don't say that." Nellie twisted to look up at Corbin.

"Oh, I'll say it," he replied, as he led her to the vehicle.

"Why?" she asked. "What still needs sorting?"

"Not a whole lot, but you know, just in case, I think I need to stick around and keep an eye on you."

Her smile started slowly and then finally burst out into joyous laughter. "You know what? I think that's probably a good idea. My father would appreciate it too."

"Screw that," Corbin said succinctly. "I'm not looking

after you for your father's sake."

"Do you have time off? Or are you leaving tomorrow?"

"Yes and no. I have time off until the next job, but I'll be managing that one from behind the scenes. This job was my commitment to going down this pathway."

"Interesting," she murmured. "Then do you get to have a break?"

"That's the plan. Potentially long-term too." He helped her into the truck, then walked around to the driver's side.

He drove them to her apartment. When she got out, she looked around. "I wasn't even sure I'd get back here again."

"Not even an issue now. Come on. Let's get you upstairs." And, with that, he held out a hand, and they walked up to her apartment.

When she looked at her front door, she turned to him. "I don't have my keys on me. I don't even know where my purse is or my laptop."

"We'll sort that out tomorrow. Right now it's sleepy time."

She looked over at him, worried to see how close he was to crashing. "You're really exhausted."

"It's been pretty strenuous these past three days."

She nodded, only to realize that he had picked the lock and was holding the door open for her. "Should I be concerned about this skill of yours?"

"Not likely. Unless you're worried that I *won't* be there to open doors for you the next time you forget your keys," he said in a dry tone, startling a laugh out of her.

"Nope, definitely not my concern, especially after everything I've been through. There's nothing like prioritizing the madness in your world."

"Especially when you're lucky enough to survive and to

make those changes."

On that note, she remembered her guard, the latest one, the off-duty cop. She stopped and asked Corbin, "The guard?"

"The one at the export warehouse will be fine. The guard you had earlier at the safe house, he didn't make it though."

She sucked in her breath. "God. So many deaths over what?"

"Money. It's almost always about money."

She didn't even know what to say about that; it just sounded so wrong. As they got into her apartment, she looked around and cried out. "Oh, my God, it's such a joy to be home."

"What do you want to do first?"

"I need food. I need a shower, and I need sleep."

"In that order?"

She frowned. "Well, I could do with the shower first, before I crash."

"You're safe here, so, if you're okay with it, I'll go to that couch and crash."

But her couch was a loveseat and not even close to accommodating him comfortably, so she shook her head. "No, head to my bed. You need real sleep, not just crashing on the couch for a few hours."

He frowned, and she waved her hand. "Go. I'll have a shower, and then I'll lay down beside you."

"Fine, but make sure that you don't go anywhere and that you don't call anyone. Not even for a food delivery."

"I can't even call anyone?" she asked, staring at him. "Not that I have my cell phone ..."

"Not yet. Not until my brain is working and I can sift

my way through what we still have to do."

"Are you just trying to keep me safe?" she murmured.

"Keeping you safe is one thing. ... I think it's all good, but I haven't had confirmation from my team yet."

"Don't worry. I would only contact my father, and he knows where we're at."

"Exactly," he muttered. He walked into the bedroom. "If you're okay, I would love a shower first but ..." He stripped off his outer layer, and he soon stood in his boxers, while he laid down on her bed and was out almost immediately.

She stared, wondering at a man who could completely relax to that extent. When a knock came on her front door, she jumped, then calmed herself down. She peeked through the peephole and saw Aiden. She opened the door and held up her finger. "He's crashed. He's on the bed, completely out."

"Good," he murmured. "I just brought his gear and some food for you guys. I'm heading to a hotel not far away here."

"Do you want to sleep here?"

He looked at the couch, shook his head. "Hell no."

She laughed. "Good call. I'll have a shower and crash myself."

"Okay, we'll talk in the morning," he said, with a gentle smile. "Take good care of him." And he was gone before she had a chance to really realize what he'd meant. Not that she had any intention of doing anything other than that. Corbin had looked after her so well that the least she could do would be to return the favor.

CORBIN OPENED HIS eyes, quickly sorted out where he was, his gaze landing on Nellie, as she'd curled up in some flimsy nightie on the bed beside him. Completely uncovered. He reached for a blanket to flip it over her shoulders, when she murmured, "I'm already hot. Don't cover me up."

He smiled and leaned over, wrapped his arms around her and pulled her back gently. She grabbed his hand and gently stroked it down to her belly. "Not exactly what I expected."

"No, me neither."

"Are you sure you're okay with this?"

"Of course I'm okay. After all that death, this is a new life, a new beginning."

"But ..." she started.

"I'm not so shallow as that. I'm not so egotistical either. And I'm not so selfish to expect anything other than for you to be delighted with the child you're carrying. Life happens. In this case, you made it happen. I won't argue with that either."

She smiled. "It could be a little bit rough to start off a relationship like this though."

"I don't know. Maybe ... we're just picking up where we left off from twenty years ago."

She slowly rolled over. "You do remember, don't you?"

He grinned at her. "You mean, the fact that you were all over me?"

"Yeah, but, as you well know, I was *ten*."

"You were an adorable ten." He grinned at her eye roll. "I think I was a whole lot older, ... eleven, at the time."

She shook her head. "As I remember, you told me that you'd come back for me."

"Sure, I was trying to be that knight in shining armor."

"I was too sad and too frightened and too devastated to

fully realize what had happened."

"And I knew that. What I didn't know, believe me, got hounded into me by my parents back then ..."

"Right, everybody was affected, weren't they?"

"Of course they were. At the time, I told my parents that I wanted to see you again, but they weren't having anything to do with that. I think in some ways they didn't want our connection to be grounded around a deadly fire."

"I was just trying to find something good to come out of something so tragic." She looked at him, puzzled.

"I know, and they had to know that too. However, after that, I was determined to join the navy and becoming a navy SEAL," he murmured against her throat. "Now I'm currently in an exit strategy."

"Does that mean that you might be around a little more often?"

"It's possible. It all depends on arrangements I make from here on in."

"Because I certainly wouldn't object to that," she muttered.

"No, maybe not. But that part of my life is still in the realm of mystery. I, on the other hand, would love to see you regardless." He looked at her steadily. "And, yes, I know you're carrying a child. But it's *your* child. It's not another man's child in that sense." He wondered if she understood that, and she did immediately.

"You know what? That's a distinction I can get behind too. Maybe it's why I was so determined to go in this direction."

"It doesn't matter what made you go in this direction. It's all good."

She smiled, "Are you ... always this reasonable?"

"Hell no."

She burst out laughing. "Okay then." She grinned. "Just checking."

He sighed softly. "Sometimes fate intervenes, and we don't exactly know why, but I'm willing to go with the flow and see where this takes us."

"I absolutely am too, although a teensy part of me has possibly been looking for you all these years."

"I doubt it." He chuckled. "I was a gangly pimply-faced kid."

"You were a hero." She swooped her arms around his neck. "You were *my* hero."

"I won't argue with that." And he leaned over and kissed her gently. "Now do you need more sleep or food? Or what do you need to do for that lovely child you're carrying?"

"This child is totally fine right now, although I will need food down the road."

"When you say, *down the road*, what does that mean?"

She frowned. "I'm not exactly sure, but I would say that I could potentially eat in another hour or two." She looked at her bedside clock and winced. "Although it is already six p.m."

"It is. Do you want to order in?"

"Is that okay? Have you cleared the decks in your mind, and we can use the phone again?"

He chuckled. "I'm glad you understood. If there had been any problems, I would know by now. And, yes, we can call in an order, now that I'm rested up."

"Yeah, that would be good. I've got a craving for Chinese."

"Do you have a favorite place?"

"Absolutely." She got out of bed and brought the menu

back to him. They quickly picked out what they wanted and placed an order.

He looked at her and grinned. "So ..."

She raised an eyebrow. "So, what?"

"What do you want to do for an hour?"

She looked at him and giggled. "I always assumed that being pregnant would be a complete turnoff."

He frowned and shook his head. "Why? This is Mother Nature at her best."

She stared at him in shock. "Seriously?"

"Of course seriously. You're a fertility goddess. You're gorgeous, and you're definitely hot."

"If you even dare say *fat*," she warned, placing her fingers against his lips.

He chuckled. "I would never say that."

"Maybe, I feel ..." She hesitated.

"Pregnant, stressed? Are you worried that you aren't sexy? Because you're wrong there. This isn't just about bodies. This is about the whole package, our souls."

She smiled and nodded. "I really like the way you think."

"Good," he stated. "I'll repeat it then. To me, life is beyond the basics of physical form. You and I have the makings of something very special together. I'd like to start the right way."

"And what is that way?" she asked hesitantly.

He looked over at her and smiled. "Well, I missed out on all the fun in getting you pregnant, but that doesn't mean I have to lose out on the fun of exploring a very pregnant body."

She stared at him. "This is really sexy to you, isn't it?"

He took her hand, drew it down his body, and asked,

"What do you think?"

She gasped at the massive erection waiting for her. "My God," and she started to giggle once more.

And, with that, he whispered, "You're beautiful. There's nothing quite like a fertile woman blooming in the fullness of a pregnancy to make every man realize that what they always wanted was to have a wife and a child."

She stared at him in shock. He reached down, kissed her gently on the cheek, and then on the lips. She shook her head. "My God, I never even thought that pregnancy would trigger sexual desires."

He chuckled. "More than triggered." He lowered his head and kissed her passionately.

She shuddered under the onslaught. As he stroked and caressed her body, until she was writhing in absolute passion, she whispered, "I still think I was waiting for you."

"Good, I'm glad we finally reconnected then."

And this time he lifted the gentle weight of her full breasts and whispered, "These are gorgeous." She shook her head, and he placed his finger against her lips. "Yes, they are."

He lowered his head and gently suckled. She almost felt like milk was coming down her breast, and she twisted in embarrassment. But he quickly moved his caring touch to her other breast, until she was completely mindless to what he was doing.

She moaned gently under his ministrations. "Dear God. I'd forgotten how wonderful this can be."

"Good," he murmured. "Then it's up to me to remind you." And, with that, he spread her thighs and gently slipped his fingers down to the plump lips below.

She twisted, trying to get closer to him, to meet the rising pressure on the inside. "Oh, my God, I need you so much right now."

"Well, it's a good thing because I wasn't planning on going anywhere."

She chuckled. "In that case you want to take care of this because I don't think I can handle much more."

And, with that, he slipped between her thighs, looked down at her, and asked, "Are you ready?"

"Oh, yeah, I'm ready." And gently he started to penetrate her, but she wasn't up for gentle. "I won't break," she said firmly. "And Baby will be fine." He hesitated, but she shook her head. "My doctor said so. You have to trust me on this because otherwise you're killing me."

He chuckled and drove himself right to the heart of her. She twisted, as if impaled, and gasped in his arms. "Are you sure you and Baby are okay?" he asked, his voice gritty.

"We're fine," she murmured, "It's just so ..." And words failed her.

"I know. Me too." And he started to move. He raised his hips, plunged deep, and then raised and lowered several more times, picking up the pace with each movement. She felt everything tightening within her, until finally an explosion reverberated inside.

He picked up his pace, groaning at his own release. He slowly collapsed beside her, careful to not hurt her. "You all right?"

She slid her hands up his chest to the back of his neck and whispered, "Never better. I can't believe I waited so long for that."

"Sorry, I guess you should have gotten yourself kidnapped a little earlier."

She burst out laughing, looking up at him, a big smile

on her face. "You do realize that it feels like I've been waiting for you since forever?"

"Yep," he said. "I haven't been able to think of anything else, since I heard what happened and realized who you were."

"You were just waiting for another chance to rescue me."

"Well, obviously the timing wasn't right for us at the first fire," he said, with a grin, as he shifted on the bed, pulling her into his arms.

"This is our time now, though."

"Yep, and Baby's." And he gently placed a hand on her belly, hesitant at first, as if asking for permission.

She smiled and covered his hand with hers.

With that, he yawned again.

"I need food before we go back to sleep." And then she remembered. "*Aiden*. He came when you were out too."

"Oh, good. Did he bring my gear? I still need that shower. A change of clothes would help too."

"He did. I didn't even think about it, but he brought food."

He leaned over and looked at her. "What did he bring?"

"I didn't even open the bags. Wow, you have a really crazy effect on me."

"That's all right. It just means that we won't have to go out for a few days."

She laughed. "That completely suits me."

He grinned. "Now ... maybe we should go check out what food Aiden brought."

"And then maybe we can come back to bed?" she asked hopefully. "At least once we eat."

He waggled his eyebrows at her. "Absolutely. I don't plan on going anywhere for the next couple days, do you?"

"To the kitchen, to the bathroom, to the bedroom. That's the extent of my upcoming travels."

"I can match that. We both need this downtime."

"You're right." Now she yawned. "The only thing would be if Jewel wants us to visit."

"She won't be leaving the hospital anytime soon. She's pretty injured, but we can call her tomorrow."

"Right. So, in that case, we can just stay here and relax."

He looped his arms around her neck, kissed her gently, and asked. "Forever?"

"Hey, if you can make that happen"—she laughed— "I'm totally on board."

He chuckled. "I have a cabin about an hour away. I thought maybe we could spend another couple weeks hibernating there."

"I'm all for that. Depends on your job though, doesn't it?"

"Depends if I can get decent internet there too. ... Otherwise we would be just fine. We can also push cabin time back until my obligations with the Mavericks are done too. As long as we're close enough to a hospital, if Baby decides to come early, we should be good."

She smiled. "And after that?"

"After that, you know me. I'm up for anything."

"That sounds wonderful."

And she reached up and kissed him gently.

Life is gonna be good.

EPILOGUE

AIDEN BRONTE WALKED into his bedroom and stretched. The last few days had been calm, relaxing, and he'd even spent some time with family. Hearing the phone ring, he looked to see who it was. "Hey, Mom."

"How are you doing? Wanted to tell you that your dad and I decided to take a cruise next month."

"Good," he said, and then he frowned. "Isn't that like short notice?"

"I think that's why your father wants to do it. There was an incredible deal, and he wants to go."

"Sounds good. Besides, I don't know where I'll be next month anyway."

"Ah, so that means you can't come with us then."

"Well, I don't know that I can or I can't, but I would say it's probably a no."

"Right."

But she didn't appear to be concerned; in fact, she appeared to be more than excited.

"If there's a chance to see you over the next couple days, it would be nice."

"I'm kinda on call, Mom. We'll see." Their call was over soon, and he got up and had a quick shower. When he came out, he'd missed a call. He immediately dialed, and, when Corbin answered the phone, Aiden asked, "Hey, you guys surviving?"

"More than surviving." Corbin yawned. "Playing house is great. You should try it."

"Even though she's got a baby coming?"

"Absolutely. You know me. I never really figured I would have a family at all. So this is just fine."

"Good. So why the call? What's going on?"

"What's going on is you're shipping out."

"I am?"

"You are. You ready?"

"Hell, yes. Do I get anybody partnered with me?"

"Well, you do, but, in this case, I'm not so sure how that'll work. Do you remember Mountain? Mountain Bear Rode?"

Mountain was one of those huge monster-size guys. "Of course. Who doesn't?"

"He's supposed to be coming on board with the Mavericks too."

"Really? I thought the Mavericks were getting their budget slashed. Also I thought Mountain was heading back up north. Canada or someplace?"

"I think something's afoot with the Mavericks. I'm not exactly sure what's going on."

"Interesting," Aiden said, with a quick frown. "That's fine, as long as I fulfill my obligation, then I'm free and clear, right?"

"You are, indeed. And believe me. I've got Nellie here trying to get me out of it too."

"Yeah, especially now that you've got a family on the way," he said in a teasing note.

"You're absolutely right, but Mountain has a different issue altogether, and he needs us. I'm not sure what that deal is, but he's coming on board to help you first, and you'll be helping him out too. I just don't have all the details."

"Where am I going?" He quickly dressed, while he was talking on the phone.

"You're leaving in twenty minutes. Mountain will be there, with wheels."

"And where are we going?"

"Vegas."

"Vegas? What's in Vegas?" He was stunned at that location. He'd only been stateside for a few days as it was.

"A series of loan sharks involved in gambling, and a supposedly innocent victim of it all."

"Yeah, in Vegas is there such a thing?"

"It looks like somebody is laundering money."

"Hardly our deal either." He frowned. "This sounds bizarre for us."

"Just like my mission, sometimes strange things happen."

"Fine. What's going on?"

"The innocent victim is our card dealer, Toby. She's been charged with murder, released on bail. I am told that she's at home in isolation."

"And we care, why?"

"Well, for one, this is not so much a paid job as it's something to do with Mountain. Hopefully he'll tell you more when he picks you up."

"Is it personal?"

"Very, but also something else." Corbin sounded frustrated, which was unusual and unnerving.

"Okay," Aiden said slowly, "that's just confusing."

"I know. Sorry. I'm not trying to be cryptic, but I'm just not getting very much in the way of intel either."

"Hey, that's not how we're supposed to work."

"I know. Believe me. Yet it has to do with Mountain."

"Fine. So I'm supposed to go to Vegas and to help solve a crime and to free somebody who is supposedly up for attempted murder charges?"

"No, not just attempted murder but first-degree murder."

"Who did she supposedly kill?"

"Her husband."

"Well, shit, that alone makes her a good suspect."

"I know, right? Everybody loves to take out their ex. But, according to her, she had nothing to do with it."

"You could have sent me anywhere in the world, and you send me to Vegas? You are going soft."

"I know. Sorry, bro. Not only that but it's not an op that we normally deal with. But, hey, lots of the cases lately have been pretty off the wall."

"If you say so," he snapped. "This is just a BS case."

"Maybe, but it's Mountain's case."

"But it's not supposed to be a Mountain case."

"I know. That's what's weird about it. Anyway he's picking you up in a few minutes. See if you can get more info out of him."

"Yeah, you can bet I will. And thanks."

"Once we're done with this case, I'd like to see you settle close to us."

"Why would you want that?"

"So you can start a family, and so we can stay friends."

"*Ha, ha.* Nobody is in my life. You know that."

"True. But I also know nobody was in my life when I did my last op too."

"No way. Somebody charged with murder doesn't sound

like my kind of partner."

"Well, that's one of many."

"What do you mean, *one of many?*"

"I think they're looking to pin four murders on her."

"Jesus Christ. Why?"

"Because they're all guys she's dealt cards to. They were at her table, winning big. Yet, when they were found, dead, no winnings were on them."

"So where's the money then?"

"Believe me. That's something that everyone would like to know. So add it to your list. Find out where the money went."

"Great," he muttered. "I'm out."

And with that, he grabbed his travel bag he'd had ready since returning from his last job and locked the front door. He walked down to the curb. He hadn't even dropped his bag when Mountain drove up in a military jeep. Aiden took one look, smiled, threw his bag in the back, and laughed. "The only reason you got a jeep is because you can have the roof off and not hit your head."

Mountain looked at him, and something in his icy gaze warmed slightly. He gave a clipped nod and said, "Nice to see your sense of humor is still there."

"Well, mine is. Where's yours?"

"Frozen," he snapped, "but I'll give you the details on the drive."

"You better," he said, settling into the passenger seat, "because I'm a little confused what kind of a deal this is."

"In a way you got the lucky job, as you might not even have to assist on the next one," he said, "because I've got something going on in the background that's big. It's deep. It's dark, and I need big-time help. Only no one believes we've got a problem, ... yet."

"Good enough," Aiden said. "You know me. I'm always there for the rescue."

This concludes Book 17 of The Mavericks: Corbin.

Read about Aiden: The Mavericks, Book 18

Aiden: Maverick (Book #18)

What happens when the very men—trained to make the hard decisions—come up against the rules and regulations that hold them back from doing what needs to be done? They either stay and work within the constraints given to them or they walk away. Only now, for a select few, they have another option:

The Mavericks. A covert black ops team that steps up and break all the rules ... but gets the job done.

Welcome to a new military romance series by *USA Today* best-selling author Dale Mayer. A series where you meet new friends and just might get to meet old ones too in this raw and compelling look at the men who keep us safe every day from the darkness where they operate—and live—in the shadows ... until someone special helps them step into the light.

Aiden has high hopes for his own mission, but Las Vegas and a woman accused of killing her own husband wasn't it. Then he finds out it's a special request from a man he's long respected and that the woman in question was his cousin.

Even more confusing is the series of other murders that, according to the local law enforcement, are linked to her as well.

Toby's life has been one long nightmare, and, just when a light shines in to save her, and she hopes she will survive this after all, the cops decide she's the one who murdered her husband. Hardly ... but, if she'd had the guts and the lack of concern for spending the rest of her life in jail for getting justice, then she'd have done it.

But, as it was, if they can't figure out who and what is going on, she'll be spending her life in prison regardless. And that would be a shame, considering she'd just met Aiden, one of the most interesting men to cross her path. Now if only he'd been here years ago, before her world went off the rails ...

Find book 18 here!
To find out more visit Dale Mayer's website.
https://geni.us/DMAidenUniversal

Author's Note

Thank you for reading Corbin: The Mavericks, Book 17! If you enjoyed the book, please take a moment and leave a short review.

Dear reader,

I love to hear from readers, and you can contact me at my website: www.dalemayer.com or at my Facebook author page. To be informed of new releases and special offers, sign up for my newsletter or follow me on BookBub. And if you are interested in joining Dale Mayer's Reader Group, here is the Facebook sign up page.
http://geni.us/DaleMayerFBGroup

Cheers,
Dale Mayer

About the Author

Dale Mayer is a *USA Today* best-selling author, best known for her SEALs military romances, her Psychic Visions series, and her Lovely Lethal Garden cozy series. Her contemporary romances are raw and full of passion and emotion (Broken But ... Mending, Hathaway House series). Her thrillers will keep you guessing (Kate Morgan, By Death series), and her romantic comedies will keep you giggling (*It's a Dog's Life*, a stand-alone novella; and the Broken Protocols series, starring Charming Marvin, the cat).

Dale honors the stories that come to her—and some of them are crazy, break all the rules and cross multiple genres!

To go with her fiction, she also writes nonfiction in many different fields, with books available on résumé writing, companion gardening, and the US mortgage system. All her books are available in print and ebook format.

Connect with Dale Mayer Online

Dale's Website – www.dalemayer.com
Twitter – @DaleMayer
Facebook Page – geni.us/DaleMayerFBFanPage
Facebook Group – geni.us/DaleMayerFBGroup
BookBub – geni.us/DaleMayerBookbub
Instagram – geni.us/DaleMayerInstagram
Goodreads – geni.us/DaleMayerGoodreads
Newsletter – geni.us/DaleNews

Also by Dale Mayer

Published Adult Books:

Shadow Recon
Magnus, Book 1

Bullard's Battle
Ryland's Reach, Book 1
Cain's Cross, Book 2
Eton's Escape, Book 3
Garret's Gambit, Book 4
Kano's Keep, Book 5
Fallon's Flaw, Book 6
Quinn's Quest, Book 7
Bullard's Beauty, Book 8
Bullard's Best, Book 9
Bullard's Battle, Books 1–2
Bullard's Battle, Books 3–4
Bullard's Battle, Books 5–6
Bullard's Battle, Books 7–8

Terkel's Team
Damon's Deal, Book 1
Wade's War, Book 2
Gage's Goal, Book 3
Calum's Contact, Book 4
Rick's Road, Book 5

Kate Morgan

Simon Says... Hide, Book 1
Simon Says... Jump, Book 2
Simon Says... Ride, Book 3
Simon Says... Scream, Book 4
Simon Says... Run, Book 5

Hathaway House

Aaron, Book 1
Brock, Book 2
Cole, Book 3
Denton, Book 4
Elliot, Book 5
Finn, Book 6
Gregory, Book 7
Heath, Book 8
Iain, Book 9
Jaden, Book 10
Keith, Book 11
Lance, Book 12
Melissa, Book 13
Nash, Book 14
Owen, Book 15
Percy, Book 16
Quinton, Book 17
Hathaway House, Books 1–3
Hathaway House, Books 4–6
Hathaway House, Books 7–9

The K9 Files

Ethan, Book 1
Pierce, Book 2
Zane, Book 3

Blaze, Book 4

Lucas, Book 5

Parker, Book 6

Carter, Book 7

Weston, Book 8

Greyson, Book 9

Rowan, Book 10

Caleb, Book 11

Kurt, Book 12

Tucker, Book 13

Harley, Book 14

Kyron, Book 15

Jenner, Book 16

The K9 Files, Books 1–2

The K9 Files, Books 3–4

The K9 Files, Books 5–6

The K9 Files, Books 7–8

The K9 Files, Books 9–10

The K9 Files, Books 11–12

Lovely Lethal Gardens

Arsenic in the Azaleas, Book 1

Bones in the Begonias, Book 2

Corpse in the Carnations, Book 3

Daggers in the Dahlias, Book 4

Evidence in the Echinacea, Book 5

Footprints in the Ferns, Book 6

Gun in the Gardenias, Book 7

Handcuffs in the Heather, Book 8

Ice Pick in the Ivy, Book 9

Jewels in the Juniper, Book 10

Killer in the Kiwis, Book 11

Lifeless in the Lilies, Book 12
Murder in the Marigolds, Book 13
Nabbed in the Nasturtiums, Book 14
Offed in the Orchids, Book 15
Poison in the Pansies, Book 16
Quarry in the Quince, Book 17
Revenge in the Roses, Book 18
Lovely Lethal Gardens, Books 1–2
Lovely Lethal Gardens, Books 3–4
Lovely Lethal Gardens, Books 5–6
Lovely Lethal Gardens, Books 7–8
Lovely Lethal Gardens, Books 9–10

Psychic Vision Series

Tuesday's Child
Hide 'n Go Seek
Maddy's Floor
Garden of Sorrow
Knock Knock...
Rare Find
Eyes to the Soul
Now You See Her
Shattered
Into the Abyss
Seeds of Malice
Eye of the Falcon
Itsy-Bitsy Spider
Unmasked
Deep Beneath
From the Ashes
Stroke of Death
Ice Maiden

Snap, Crackle…
What If…
Talking Bones
Psychic Visions Books 1–3
Psychic Visions Books 4–6
Psychic Visions Books 7–9

By Death Series
Touched by Death
Haunted by Death
Chilled by Death
By Death Books 1–3

Broken Protocols – Romantic Comedy Series
Cat's Meow
Cat's Pajamas
Cat's Cradle
Cat's Claus
Broken Protocols 1-4

Broken and… Mending
Skin
Scars
Scales (of Justice)
Broken but… Mending 1-3

Glory
Genesis
Tori
Celeste
Glory Trilogy

Biker Blues

Morgan: Biker Blues, Volume 1

Cash: Biker Blues, Volume 2

SEALs of Honor

Mason: SEALs of Honor, Book 1

Hawk: SEALs of Honor, Book 2

Dane: SEALs of Honor, Book 3

Swede: SEALs of Honor, Book 4

Shadow: SEALs of Honor, Book 5

Cooper: SEALs of Honor, Book 6

Markus: SEALs of Honor, Book 7

Evan: SEALs of Honor, Book 8

Mason's Wish: SEALs of Honor, Book 9

Chase: SEALs of Honor, Book 10

Brett: SEALs of Honor, Book 11

Devlin: SEALs of Honor, Book 12

Easton: SEALs of Honor, Book 13

Ryder: SEALs of Honor, Book 14

Macklin: SEALs of Honor, Book 15

Corey: SEALs of Honor, Book 16

Warrick: SEALs of Honor, Book 17

Tanner: SEALs of Honor, Book 18

Jackson: SEALs of Honor, Book 19

Kanen: SEALs of Honor, Book 20

Nelson: SEALs of Honor, Book 21

Taylor: SEALs of Honor, Book 22

Colton: SEALs of Honor, Book 23

Troy: SEALs of Honor, Book 24

Axel: SEALs of Honor, Book 25

Baylor: SEALs of Honor, Book 26

Hudson: SEALs of Honor, Book 27

Lachlan: SEALs of Honor, Book 28
Paxton: SEALs of Honor, Book 29
SEALs of Honor, Books 1–3
SEALs of Honor, Books 4–6
SEALs of Honor, Books 7–10
SEALs of Honor, Books 11–13
SEALs of Honor, Books 14–16
SEALs of Honor, Books 17–19
SEALs of Honor, Books 20–22
SEALs of Honor, Books 23–25

Heroes for Hire

Levi's Legend: Heroes for Hire, Book 1
Stone's Surrender: Heroes for Hire, Book 2
Merk's Mistake: Heroes for Hire, Book 3
Rhodes's Reward: Heroes for Hire, Book 4
Flynn's Firecracker: Heroes for Hire, Book 5
Logan's Light: Heroes for Hire, Book 6
Harrison's Heart: Heroes for Hire, Book 7
Saul's Sweetheart: Heroes for Hire, Book 8
Dakota's Delight: Heroes for Hire, Book 9
Tyson's Treasure: Heroes for Hire, Book 10
Jace's Jewel: Heroes for Hire, Book 11
Rory's Rose: Heroes for Hire, Book 12
Brandon's Bliss: Heroes for Hire, Book 13
Liam's Lily: Heroes for Hire, Book 14
North's Nikki: Heroes for Hire, Book 15
Anders's Angel: Heroes for Hire, Book 16
Reyes's Raina: Heroes for Hire, Book 17
Dezi's Diamond: Heroes for Hire, Book 18
Vince's Vixen: Heroes for Hire, Book 19
Ice's Icing: Heroes for Hire, Book 20

Johan's Joy: Heroes for Hire, Book 21
Galen's Gemma: Heroes for Hire, Book 22
Zack's Zest: Heroes for Hire, Book 23
Bonaparte's Belle: Heroes for Hire, Book 24
Noah's Nemesis: Heroes for Hire, Book 25
Tomas's Trials: Heroes for Hire, Book 26
Heroes for Hire, Books 1–3
Heroes for Hire, Books 4–6
Heroes for Hire, Books 7–9
Heroes for Hire, Books 10–12
Heroes for Hire, Books 13–15
Heroes for Hire, Books 16–18
Heroes for Hire, Books 19–21
Heroes for Hire, Books 22–24

SEALs of Steel
Badger: SEALs of Steel, Book 1
Erick: SEALs of Steel, Book 2
Cade: SEALs of Steel, Book 3
Talon: SEALs of Steel, Book 4
Laszlo: SEALs of Steel, Book 5
Geir: SEALs of Steel, Book 6
Jager: SEALs of Steel, Book 7
The Final Reveal: SEALs of Steel, Book 8
SEALs of Steel, Books 1–4
SEALs of Steel, Books 5–8
SEALs of Steel, Books 1–8

The Mavericks
Kerrick, Book 1
Griffin, Book 2
Jax, Book 3
Beau, Book 4

Asher, Book 5

Ryker, Book 6

Miles, Book 7

Nico, Book 8

Keane, Book 9

Lennox, Book 10

Gavin, Book 11

Shane, Book 12

Diesel, Book 13

Jerricho, Book 14

Killian, Book 15

Hatch, Book 16

Corbin, Book 17

Aiden, Book 18

The Mavericks, Books 1–2

The Mavericks, Books 3–4

The Mavericks, Books 5–6

The Mavericks, Books 7–8

The Mavericks, Books 9–10

The Mavericks, Books 11–12

Collections

Dare to Be You…

Dare to Love…

Dare to be Strong…

RomanceX3

Standalone Novellas

It's a Dog's Life

Riana's Revenge

Second Chances

Published Young Adult Books:

Family Blood Ties Series
Vampire in Denial
Vampire in Distress
Vampire in Design
Vampire in Deceit
Vampire in Defiance
Vampire in Conflict
Vampire in Chaos
Vampire in Crisis
Vampire in Control
Vampire in Charge
Family Blood Ties Set 1–3
Family Blood Ties Set 1–5
Family Blood Ties Set 4–6
Family Blood Ties Set 7–9
Sian's Solution, A Family Blood Ties Series Prequel
    Novelette

Design series
Dangerous Designs
Deadly Designs
Darkest Designs
Design Series Trilogy

Standalone
In Cassie's Corner
Gem Stone (a Gemma Stone Mystery)
Time Thieves

Published Non-Fiction Books:

Career Essentials
Career Essentials: The Résumé
Career Essentials: The Cover Letter
Career Essentials: The Interview
Career Essentials: 3 in 1

Printed in Great Britain
by Amazon

58724047R00134